NEWS OF OUR LOVED ONES

Center Point
Large Print

**This Large Print Book carries the
Seal of Approval of N.A.V.H.**

NEWS OF OUR LOVED ONES

ABIGAIL DeWITT

CENTER POINT LARGE PRINT
THORNDIKE, MAINE

This Center Point Large Print edition
is published in the year 2019 by arrangement with
Harper, an imprint of HarperCollins Publishers.

The text of this Large Print edition is unabridged.
In other aspects, this book may vary
from the original edition.
Printed in the United States of America
on permanent paper.
Set in 16-point Times New Roman type.

ISBN: 978-1-64358-059-3

Library of Congress Cataloging-in-Publication Data

Names: De Witt, Abigail, author.
Title: News of our loved ones / Abigail DeWitt.
Description: Large Print edition. | Thorndike, Maine :
    Center Point Large Print, 2019.
Identifiers: LCCN 2018045868 | ISBN 9781643580593
    (hardcover : alk. paper)
Subjects: LCSH: Large type books. | Families—Fiction. |
    GSAFD: War stories.
Classification: LCC PS3554.E92937 N49 2019 | DDC 813/.54—dc23
LC record available at https://lccn.loc.gov/2018045868

*In memory of my mother,
Cécile DeWitt-Morette,
and for Sarah.*

To go home, one must become a refugee.

—Tim O'Brien, *Going After Cacciato*

CONTENTS

THE WAR

AFTER THE WAR

THE WAR

LIBERATION

Sirens. Was that what she'd heard? Yvonne dreamed about air raids when there weren't any, slept soundly through the actual warnings. At first, every siren sent the whole family racing to the cellar; they crouched together in the dark, making themselves as small as possible, their faces hidden in their knees. But after a while, they gave up going downstairs. Yvonne and her sisters, Françoise and Geneviève, climbed into Maman's bed, burrowing into the warmth of her covers; their stepfather, Oncle Henri, paced the room. Then even that was too much trouble. There was only so much fear a body could hold. If Yvonne heard anything during the night now, she pulled the pillow over her head.

The hunger was worse, the craving for beef, pork, butter most of all. She wanted butter and marmalade on toast, buttery croissants still warm from the patisserie, a butter and ham sandwich, Maman's *kouign amann.*

It did seem to her that there had been sirens during the night, but who could say? She didn't always hear things the way other people did. The confusion never lasted long, but there were moments when the buzzing of a mosquito sounded louder to her than a German parade;

13

when the breathing of her classmates hurt her ears, though the teacher was inaudible.

But the question of nighttime air raids was something else: no one was sure about those anymore.

She rolled over in bed, staring at the faint ribbon of light that slipped through a crack in the shutters. She was so happy to be home, in her room with the red wallpaper and the curtains with their pattern of violets. It was the smallest room in the house, barely enough space for the bed, a child-sized armoire, and a three-legged stool. A single bookshelf hung on the wall above the armoire. Françoise's room was bigger, though she was the baby, and there were three empty rooms—her older sister, Geneviève, had moved to Paris in September, her two older brothers had left home long ago—but Françoise's room had to be reached through Maman's, and the older children's rooms, though light and airy, were at the back of the house. Yvonne preferred this one, with its balcony overlooking the street.

She and Françoise had been sent home from school at the end of May along with the other boarders; the Allies were expected any day now and it would be better for all the girls to be with their families. Boarders wouldn't have to take exams, they wouldn't have to obey the nuns again until September. Not all of the nuns were cruel—two or three, beloved of the younger girls, were even pretty—but the ones who weren't mean were mostly stupid. Vicious or insipid, they drained the pleasure out of every bright moment.

When the Germans had come, her grandmother had pointed out at dinner that some of them weren't so bad, some had perfectly decent manners, and Oncle Henri had left the table in disgust; Yvonne, allying herself with her stepfather for the first and only time in her life, had thought, *It's the same with the nuns. It's stupid to make distinctions between them.*

She hated the nuns frankly and openly, which was possible only because Oncle Henri supplied the convent with coal, and though her boldness filled the other girls with awe, she had no illusions: if it weren't for the coal, she'd be as obedient as the next girl.

When she was twelve, in answer to a question from the Mother Superior about what she was thinking, Yvonne had looked up at her without flinching. "I would like to crush you," she said, and she made a motion with her hands as if she were grinding something with a mortar and pestle. Nothing happened. The Mother Superior did not speak or move. She hardly even seemed to breathe. Yvonne would have thought she had imagined the whole thing if not for her racing heart.

But she might have imagined last night's sirens.

Any minute now, Maman would call her down

to breakfast, to a watery bowl of chicory that satisfied no craving. Why go down when her bedroom, even in the early morning gloom, was so beautiful and was hers alone? She wanted to open her shutters and breathe in the smell of honeysuckle and seagulls, of the dusty pear trees across the road, but then everyone would know she was awake and there would be no excuse for staying in bed. She gazed up at the spines of her books, at Mirabelle's lone porcelain foot sticking out from the shelf. The doll sat with the books, placed with the other *M*'s (Molière, Montesquieu) to keep things in alphabetical order. A sock dangled from Mirabelle's foot and below her stood the small armoire, with its fleur-de-lis, its fluted edges—who had done this, Yvonne wondered, carved the wood so beautifully? On the rickety stool was an old lamp, and even it, with its shade partly burned through, seemed to Yvonne a kind of miracle.

Her throat tightened. She might see him today. Why shouldn't he bicycle down the street at two o'clock as he'd always done and glance up at her balcony? She didn't know his name. She didn't even know where he had been headed every day last summer when he rode past, staring up at her. For weeks she hadn't met his gaze. She would catch sight of him, turning the corner onto their street—always between 1:50 and 2:05—his head bare, red hair ruffled by the breeze and his face open, handsome, easy. One arm dangled by his side and the other barely touched the handlebar. Instantly, she glanced down. She felt his eyes on her, felt the heat of his gaze the entire length of time it took for him to reach the end of the street—a one-minute ride that seemed to take hours—though she couldn't have known in the beginning if he even noticed her. When he was right below the house, she saw a blur in her peripheral vision, that was all.

And then one day—her heart had been sore all morning, like something she'd swallowed the wrong way—she glanced out when he would be approaching the house and he was right below her, staring up. The next day she looked again. And then for days, weeks, she stared at him the whole length of his ride and he stared back, turning to look over his shoulder when he reached the end of the street. They were the happiest days of her life, of all her sixteen years, those two weeks when, for a minute or two every afternoon, she and the red-haired boy looked nakedly at each other.

Though she was starving, she couldn't eat, and the feel of her bones pressing up through her skin thrilled her. Hip bones, clavicle, shoulder blades, jawbone: wherever her skin grew taut, she imagined his hand. The world was glazed with light and the Germans made no sound at all. *I love you,* she thought, watching him ride toward her. And even when he wasn't there: *I love you, I love you, I love you.*

She heard his voice sometimes. When she was coming out of the bathroom, while she was waiting in line for food. It was deep and sudden and always a little too close. He'd speak more softly, she thought, if he knew it hurt her. Like sandpaper on an open sore. She hadn't known that pleasure and fear were so alike.

But she was never afraid when she saw him. She stared right into his eyes, irises as blue as the early morning, and smiled at him.

And then one day, he stopped. He parked his bike in front of her house and called up. "Hello!" he said, his voice so much milder than she had imagined. He bowed. She stifled a laugh—beads of sweat were rolling down her sides—and called back, trembling: "Hello!"

That was the end of it: Oncle Henri burst through the front door, told the boy to stop gawking, went upstairs, and slapped Yvonne in full view of the street. She never met his gaze again, though for the rest of the summer she still stood on the balcony every day from 1:50 to 2:05, her mouth dry and her throat sore, staring at him. She prayed for him to look up, to see her suffering, to know that she loved him, but he looked straight ahead. The day before she went back to school at the end of the summer, she whistled a tune from childhood as soon as he appeared on the street, but he didn't glance up. The whistle died in her throat and the only sound was the whisper of his tires on the pavement. And then, in front of the house, he paused. He climbed off his bicycle, slipped something under a rock, climbed back on, and vanished.

That evening, just before curfew, when the street was nearly dark, she slipped out and found his note. *You are a bird.*

That was all. She read it over and over and gave it a thousand meanings, seeing in the slope of his letters such declarations of love, such caresses, but that's all it was, the four words, *tu es un oiseau.* The *tu* was everything, as if they'd already kissed, as if he had already cupped his hand around the back of her neck and pulled her toward him, pressed his lips against hers; as if she had already smelled him, felt the coolness of his body, the muscles of his hands, as if she had felt her teeth press against the inside of her lips as they did when she pressed her own palm to her mouth, imagining. The *tu* and the bird, that she was a bird, that he should say so, the knowledge of her so intimate. But what could she say in return? She stayed up late, composing a long letter in which she described not only the depth of her love but all the members of her family and the color of her room and her hatred of the Germans and all the things they would eat together, the two of them, when the war was over.

The letter was seventeen pages long and it was three in the morning before she finished it and then she folded it up and put it in a notebook. She took a clean sheet of paper, wrote *thank you,* and, though it would kill Oncle Henri to know that she was violating curfew—putting them all at risk for her own purposes!—she slipped through the front door and left the note under the same rock where he had left his.

"Yvonne!" her mother called. "Are you still asleep?"

She closed her eyes and dozed a little.

"Yvonne!"

And then, because it was hopeless, they'd call her down no matter what now, she rose and opened her shutters and gasped at the freshness of the air, the smell of the salt, of the honeysuckle. It was not possible that the world could be so beautiful. It had rained while she slept, and the sky was still low and velvety, the color of smoke. She closed the curtains to dress and turned on the lamp: the walls turned crimson and the armoire glowed like roasting chestnuts—none of this was possible, she thought. She made up her bed, smoothing the violets on her bedspread with the flat of her palm and this, too—the bed, the motion of her own hand, seemed impossibly beautiful to her.

But Maman was waiting downstairs with a

list of chores and Yvonne must hurry or be met already—so soon into her vacation—with her mother's disapproval. (Because surely they wouldn't call the girls back to school now? Surely this was the beginning of summer vacation. Either the Allies would come and there'd be too much fighting, or they wouldn't and everyone would keep expecting them from day to day.) It was as if Maman turned to stone when she was displeased, her face suddenly cold and remote.

She hurried downstairs, hurried in the bathroom, and found her mother and Françoise at the table drinking their bowls of chicory. Oncle Henri was already weeding the garden and it struck Yvonne that, though she had wanted to stay in her room, though she loved her red walls and her armoire and had not wanted to be called down, even this—the long table, the bowls of foul liquid, her mother's sagging face and Oncle Henri's profile through the window—was more beautiful than she had ever realized. Françoise slurped her chicory, her long black braids falling down her back, her chair a little closer to Maman's than it needed to be. She was fifteen, mostly fun—she laughed at Yvonne's jokes—but she still clung to Maman, always standing slightly behind or next to her, pulling her chair closer to Maman than necessary; and Maman relied on Françoise as she never relied on Yvonne, asking her to fetch things, to unfasten the back of her dress, find the cream for her feet, even when Françoise had schoolwork to do.

Maman smiled faintly at Yvonne; she always looked tired now. "The rain's let up. I thought we'd weed the lawn around the steps."

"We might die today," Yvonne said, breezily.

Françoise, half asleep, kept her head over her bowl of chicory, forcing the liquid down with tiny, labored sips.

"Did you hear the sirens?" Maman asked.

"I think so."

"I thought so, too," Maman said, putting down her napkin though her chicory was only half drunk. "Brush your teeth, girls, and then we'll get to work."

And though it was a long time to lunch, and longer still until the hour between one and two when the family rested and Yvonne stood out on her balcony, she didn't mind weeding today. Françoise hummed mindlessly beside her, and all the flowers were blooming, the roses and the peonies and the foxglove. The heads of lettuce were full and healthy, all in their rows, and the sweet peas covered the fences. She remembered the poem she'd memorized for English, *the lark's on the wing . . . all's right with the world,* and, resting on her haunches, looking up at the dove-gray sky, she thought, *Yes. It is.* She would see him today.

Though the war raged on, though she craved

a fistful of butter, still, the damp wind silvered the leaves and the roses grew up the garden wall. And Maman, sweating beneath her hat, wordlessly taking the shears from Françoise, was beautiful, with her fat knees, her rings of sweat. Even Oncle Henri, digging at the far side of the yard, with his cold face, his list of rules and chores, was beautiful. For she was loved.

She gazed at the rust-colored stones in the wall, and at the rabbit hutch with its dark, musty smell so redolent of stew, of the rabbits' tiny pelts stitched together into coats, their bodies smooth and shiny after they'd been skinned. It had horrified her in the first winter of the war that Maman killed them and that she herself was required to skin them; the first several times she'd wept with Maman standing over her, correcting her technique—you must pull just so, so that the skin comes off in one piece—but now all she thought of was the warm, slippery meat, the soft fur, the glistening bodies, and this was not only because she was in love, but because she was ravenous after her bowl of chicory and a morning outside. And because no matter how warm she grew working in the garden, she hadn't forgotten the cold of the winter, or the chilblains she could never scratch hard enough.

For lunch they had omelets and salad, though there was no oil for the dressing, no butter for the eggs. But now she didn't mind: soon they would all take their naps, and she could go out onto her balcony.

"I'd like to talk to you both after you've finished the dishes," Maman said to Yvonne and Françoise.

"I'm so tired, Maman," Yvonne said, dry-mouthed, her throat so tight it hurt to speak. She dried the last of the plates. "Could we talk later?"

"Well, of course," said Maman. "Let's all have a nap."

Her head ached, and her throat, her heart, and the minutes passed more slowly than when, as a small child, she and Françoise had waited in the schoolyard for their mother to pick them up.

The clock struck the quarter hour and Yvonne jumped, her eyes fixed on the end of the street.

The hour came, the quarter past. He was not coming.

Maman knocked on her door. "It's late, Yvonne." And in her mother's voice, she heard the truth: they would all be dead soon. Maman had known what she was waiting for, had given her the extra fifteen minutes so that she could die happy. Maman could not have known that he wasn't coming, that—what? He'd found another girl? Moved away, died? Maman wouldn't have been watching the street all these weeks and months, she would simply have known that Yvonne would watch it as soon as she came home, and Maman would have allowed her, because they were dying; when you were dying, you could do anything.

But he hadn't come. She had waited faithfully, and he had forgotten her. She would die without him—her body revolted as if she'd swallowed something rotten: she couldn't die. Then she began to laugh, a trembling so fine it was barely more than a hum. What choice was there? Soon— in a week? A few hours? She would simply cease.

The world had seemed so vivid that morning only because she was dying. For though she had loved the boy with the red hair, though it had been delicious to feel herself loved—*tu es un oiseau*—still, the sudden beauty of the walls, of the polished wood, of her mother's sweat-stained dress—what were they but the rapture of farewell?

"I'll be right there, Maman." She turned from the balcony and, without thinking, almost pulled the shutters closed, the windows, as if it were time for bed. Her chest burned, but her mother was waiting for her, with her kind, sagging face, her fat arms. Yvonne opened the door, and there was Maman, white with irritation. She wasn't thinking of death at all.

The boy with the red hair did not love her, her mother's face was stiff and disapproving as a nun's (more so, because no one gave Maman extra coal). They would be dead soon and everyone went on with his work, as if it were a day like any other, as if it meant nothing at all to leave the honeysuckle, the sea cliffs, the footless leg of Mirabelle.

"It's too late to have the talk I wanted to have with you," Maman said, sharply. "Oncle Henri wants you to get right to your studies."

But what could Maman have wanted to talk about, since apparently, she realized neither that Yvonne was in love, nor that they were going to be killed soon? Yvonne's behavior at school? The need to economize? The coming chores? She reached up on impulse and put her palm to Maman's cheek. "I'm sorry I overslept, petite Maman," she said, and kissed her.

Maybe it was better this way, with no one knowing.

Oncle Henri sat beside her and Françoise while they studied to make sure that their eyes did not stray to the open windows. Montaigne said, *My life has been filled with terrible misfortune, most of which never happened,* and the cool smell of the garden washed over her and she glanced at the dark hairs on the backs of Oncle Henri's hands and the braids down Françoise's back—how steadily they both read—and she would have kissed them, too, except that she didn't want to startle them.

In the night, hearing bombs and sure they wouldn't live till morning, Yvonne crawled into her mother's bed.

"What is it?" Maman asked sleepily.

"I was afraid."

"Yvonne?" Maman asked, waking fully. "I thought you were Françoise. What are you doing here?"

"A bad dream."

"Sh-sh," said Maman. "You're too big." But she put her arm around Yvonne, and Yvonne curled into her soft, faintly sour body.

The next day dawned more beautifully than the last—the clouds, all violet and gray, were blowing off—and Yvonne, hastily dressing in the room she loved so much, saw no reason why they should die that day or why the boy with the red hair, belatedly learning that the convent had sent all its pupils home, should not come by after all.

She went down to her bowl of chicory and gaily refused to brush her teeth after, because, she laughed—the joke never grew old—they might be dead by nightfall.

Maman sighed: there was an awful lot of work to be done. The windows hadn't been washed in a month and there was a rabbit to kill.

Yvonne stood on her balcony after lunch, staring down at the end of the street, and though she imagined a hundred reasons why he might not show up—why should he have heard that the convent had sent the girls home?—her arms trembled at her sides and she felt as if she would be sick.

The clock struck one thirty and though he'd never come that early, not once, the sound of the planes overhead became confused in her mind with the whisper of his bicycle tires, so that it was only as her clothes burst into flames that she gave up hoping it was he.

NEWS OF OUR LOVED ONES

The sun was perfectly still, a white hole in the middle of the sky. The other mothers had collected their daughters long ago, but my mother was always late. She was very busy, because my father had been sick in bed for years, and my sisters, Yvonne and Françoise, were still in diapers, and there was the whole garden to tend to, the eggs to collect, the rabbit cages to clean, so many chores! My older brothers, Louis and Simon, could walk to and from school by themselves, but I was not allowed to go out in the street alone.

Sister John of the Cross opened the door and called out to me, "You don't need to cling to the gate like a little convict, your mother will be here soon enough. Do you need to use the latrine?" I stopped hopping from foot to foot and went to the other side of the yard where the benches were. I could not risk going to the latrine. Suppose Maman came while I was squatting down and I didn't see her?

A cloud slipped over the sun, darkening the yard, and the gate swung open—it was Maman's sister, Tante Chouchotte. "Come, *ma pauvre*," Tante Chouchotte said. "Come, *ma chérie*." But

I was afraid to stand up. "Oh," Tante Chouchotte said, lighting a cigarette and touching the back of my dress. "It's nothing. You'll be dry before we even get home." My legs were sticky and I must have been ashamed—I was five, too old to have an accident—but I don't remember that part, only the stickiness, and the sour smell.

Tante Chouchotte walked fast, long gray hair bouncing on her shoulders. I had to run to keep up, and after a while, she threw her cigarette down and carried me. Once, I'd overheard Maman talking about Tante Chouchotte to Sister John of the Cross: Tante Chouchotte's son had drowned, her husband was killed in the war of 1914, her daughter had died of the flu when she was six weeks old. Tante Chouchotte had had to go into an asylum. She had turned her back on God. The word "asylum" meant nothing to me, of course, but I often pictured everything else: God on His throne, a soldier on a horse, a boy in the river, a coughing baby.

I was afraid of Tante Chouchotte—her voice was low and rough—but it was nice being carried above the street, bumping along. If Tante Chouchotte walked fast enough, I could see my older brothers before they went back to school for the afternoon. Simon and Louis were thirteen years old—twins—and they'd been adopted, but we weren't supposed to say so.

Grown-ups insisted it was impossible to tell

them apart, but that wasn't true: Simon was quiet and had a short leg because he'd had polio. Louis, Maman said, was too loud. He threw his ball against the side of the house, and he laughed when he wasn't supposed to. Once, he'd jumped from the cliffs near Etretat, far out into the ocean, where the waves and the rocks could kill you. Besides my mother and father, I loved Louis best of all.

I laid my head on Tante Chouchotte's shoulder, and it was like being on a horse, up and down and up and down.

When I awoke, I was in the living room, on Maman's lap, and my grandmother was crying. She cried often, because she was old. Louis and Simon were sitting on the sofa, staring at the floor. I wanted Louis to wink at me, the way he'd done before when Grandmère cried, but he wouldn't. Oncle Henri, Papa's friend, who was not our uncle, was there, too, with his hand on Maman's shoulder.

Grandmère's cries grew louder, and Maman told Tante Chouchotte she didn't need to stay. "Henri will help with the arrangements, Chouchotte. You should go back to Paris. I'll see you on Sunday for the funeral." I didn't know what a funeral was, any more than I knew about asylums, but I loved my mother's smell—warm, like the chicken shed.

Tante Chouchotte lit another cigarette.

31

"It's fine," Maman said. "You can go." She touched the cross at her neck.

"For God's sake," Tante Chouchotte said.

Maman closed her eyes the way she did when we wore her out and she wanted us all to be quiet. I asked if I could visit Papa in his room. It was what I did every day after school. Before lunch, before anything, I climbed up beside my father on his bed and kissed him. Over and over, butterfly kisses. His face was long and covered with stubble, and he smiled when I kissed him. But Oncle Henri said absolutely not, that was no place for children.

I looked up at Oncle Henri, who was staring at my mother. *I hate you,* I thought. It was a new thought, one I'd never had before, and I liked it. It was like sucking on a cool stone.

"*Ma pauvre chérie,*" Maman murmured, standing up. "Poor dear, you're all wet."

When I was seven, Oncle Henri and my mother were engaged to be married. I didn't want Oncle Henri for a stepfather, but Louis ruffled my hair and laughed. "It won't change anything. Besides," he added, "there'll be champagne, and you'll get to wear your pretty frock." I stopped worrying then. I loved the pink silk dress Maman had made for me. It was the first beautiful thing I had ever owned, and Maman, who didn't believe in frivolous things, had worked on it night after night, sewing tiny pink roses around the waist, which weren't necessary at all, just beautiful.

The house had to be cleaned for the wedding party, new bed linens bought, the cake assembled and decorated. The day before the party, Maman and I took the long way back from the market. "We'll avoid the crowds," she murmured, turning away from the main street. "We can make a little stroll of it, just the two of us, before everyone arrives for the party." We walked along the river and the salt air blew in from the coast. I skipped a little, carrying the basket with all the last-minute things: a sprig of parsley, a kilo of cherries, a new white tablecloth, and napkins with red roses embroidered along the edges.

But a motorcar sped past, raising a cloud of dust; it swerved to avoid a dog, made a thumping sound, and vanished in the distance. Maman gasped, grabbed my hand, and ran as if she meant to catch up with the car—and then she stopped and the air shifted, grew still. The skin tightened around my bones: Mademoiselle Duchaté, who gave piano lessons in her home, lay on her stomach in the ditch, her dress lifted almost to her underwear, the side of her face slick with blood. There was dirt everywhere: in her hair and on her dress, covering the bread and cheese that had spilled out of her bag.

I screamed. I kept screaming while Maman scrambled down into the ditch, put her face close to Mademoiselle Duchaté's, scrambled back out, and slapped me. "Don't be an idiot!" she said, pulling me down into the ditch. "Here." She took one of the lovely, rose-patterned napkins and pressed it to Mademoiselle's forehead. "Hold this until I get back."

Maman ran down the road, and I was alone in the ditch with Mademoiselle Duchaté. Mademoiselle Duchaté's breath came out of her in hard gasps, as if she were pushing something heavy, and warm blood seeped through the linen onto my fingertips. The air grew damp, as if it would rain, and I wanted to run after my mother, to grab her hand and go wherever she was going, but the burn of her palm print held me still. I glanced down at the blood-soaked roses, at Mademoiselle's matted hair and long, dirty nose, and I began to cry. I cried quietly at first, afraid of disturbing her, and then I cried as loudly as I could, louder than Grandmère had cried when Papa died, until my throat was raw and I was done with crying. The day hung heavy and still around us, and the only sound in the ditch now was Mademoiselle's panting, like a dog's.

An automobile drove past finally, stopped, and backed up. Maman jumped out with a couple I didn't know. The man stepped down beside me in the ditch, lifted Mademoiselle in his arms, put her in the back of the automobile, and drove away. When they were gone, Maman sighed and collected our things: the cherries and parsley and linens, the bloody napkin. She touched my face. "Fear is a form of selfishness," she said. Her voice was soft, the way it was after I'd had a nightmare. "You're a big girl now, and you must set yourself bravely to the task before you. You don't want to make a spectacle of your feelings." I looked away, my eyes burning, and pretended to search for cherries. Louis was wrong: the wedding had ruined everything, and it hadn't even happened yet.

By the time I was fifteen and war broke out with Germany, I knew how to freeze my face, the way my mother did. The newsboy was shouting down the street, my grandmother was standing in the doorway, saying, "No, no, no, no, no, no," my mother hid her face in her hands and wept, but I kept clearing the breakfast dishes as if nothing had happened. I felt a moment of scorn for my mother's display. I wasn't afraid at all. Louis still lived with us—Simon had moved to Paris, gotten married—and Louis said we could beat the *boches* in no time. He'd been saying it for weeks.

Louis raised racehorses, and in the evenings, when he came home, dirty and smelling of horse sweat, he tousled my hair and called me his favorite girl. Yvonne and Françoise were twelve and eleven, pretty girls with dark eyes and long dark braids, so alike they could have been twins themselves. Everyone praised their charm—I was pale and awkward—but I didn't mind, because Louis loved me the best. I played the violin, and though I wasn't very good, Louis stood in the door of my bedroom sometimes and clapped at every pause. What did I care that he couldn't tell the end of a movement from the end of a piece?

The day before Louis left to join the cavalry, he took me riding with him. He lifted me onto an old mare he'd retired, and we rode out past the farms and orchards west of town. The sun fell before us toward the coast, too bright to look at. Just after sunset, we stopped at the edge of Ouistreham, the horizon burnished red, and then we turned back, and followed the river home. There were women he went dancing with in the evenings, but I didn't take them seriously. In the fading light, with his thin mustache and light brown hair, he seemed to belong only to me. I wondered if, having no blood ties, we might marry in a few years. I wondered the same thing every day for the next three months, until they returned Louis's helmet and tags to us.

We lost the war. I turned sixteen, seventeen, eighteen. My sisters' beauty failed to blossom, their hair dry and thin and their bodies stunted, like the bodies of perpetual children. I kept to my room and practiced the violin, as if I could drown out every other sound: the German melodies outside my window, the noise of horses trammeling Louis into the mud. Maman wanted me to practice in the living room, where everyone could hear me—she wanted us all together—but Oncle Henri said to leave me be. He'd studied the piano when he was young, and bad playing gave him a headache. They ought to get a thicker door for my bedroom, he said.

Every week brought the announcement of a new set of rules—who could do what and where and when. An endless list of prohibitions and punishments. We stepped off the sidewalk when the *boches* passed, our gazes fixed on the pavement, and all we talked about was food: where to find it; how much it cost; what to substitute for sugar, coffee, butter, meat, flour. My stomach hurt, and I was always cold.

I began to dream that I'd done terrible things: I'd drowned the rabbits we were saving for stew, I'd dug Louis's body out of the ground. The dreams always began at the end, when it was too late to undo my crime, so that night after night, I watched the aftermath of my cravenness. The sun burned Louis's skin, and rabbits gazed at me from the bottom of a pool. In the morning, exhausted, I prayed for forgiveness.

Grandmère said the Germans were not as bad as all that—they were very well behaved—and Maman said Grandmère didn't know what she was talking about. What about the Naquets and the Schwarzes? Maman asked. Did Grandmère think they were on a cruise? "They're only Jews," Grandmère said, and Oncle Henri shoved himself away from the dinner table. But, of course, he came back. The soup might be mostly water and Grandmère senile, but we had to eat.

Maman had no patience for any of us. She threw my door open when I was practicing, insisted that I hadn't washed the potatoes well enough, hadn't properly weeded the garden. She'd demand to know why I didn't spend more time with my sisters, but my sisters had each other. They didn't need me. "You don't value your family," my mother said.

It was Oncle Henri who released me, finally, in the summer of '43. Oncle Henri! One morning at breakfast, he announced that he'd written to a friend in Paris, Jean Crunelle, professor of violin at the National Conservatory. Maître Crunelle would be happy to help me prepare an audition.

I thought he was joking. A terrible, elaborate prank, holding out the promise of freedom—but Maman froze, her face as blank as if she'd suffered a stroke.

"She can commute," Oncle Henri said, brightly. "Crunelle will arrange for her to get a pass, and she can spend the week in Paris at Chouchotte's and come back to Caen on the weekends."

"The Allies are bombing the trains," Maman said in a low, strangled voice.

"Not the passenger trains, but in any case, she can stay full-time at Chouchotte's if you prefer." *It's to get rid of me,* I thought, and I could feel my heart pounding. The long sentence of childhood was ending. I would be able to do as I pleased.

There was no room for me in Tante Chouchotte's little garret, Maman said, and when Oncle Henri said I could stay with Simon, she waved her hand impatiently. Simon's apart-ment, which she'd never seen, was also too small. "Besides," she added, "there's the baby now. Michelle's exhausted. Colic day and night. Geneviève isn't going anywhere." Maman was tone-deaf, otherwise she would have realized what Oncle Henri knew perfectly well: I'd never be admitted to the conservatory.

"A pension?" Oncle Henri suggested mildly, putting his hand on Maman's.

Tante Chouchotte was waiting for me at the station in Paris. "*Chérie,*" she said, taking my face in her hands. Whatever had once unsettled me about her moved me now: her deep, smoke-ravaged voice, her tangle of gray hair, even the gold cap that had appeared on her front tooth. She was taller and bonier than my mother, and much more brilliant—she taught literature at the Lycée Victor-Duruy—but their smiles, despite the perfect teeth of one, the gold glint of the other, were identical. And they had the same gray eyes. She was like my mother, I thought, but with none of the moralizing.

"Come," Tante Chouchotte said. "Let's get you settled." It was an overcast day, threatening rain, but the long avenues, the rows of chestnut trees, the fashionably dressed women who did not even glance at me—they hadn't known me since birth, had no opinion of me at all—made me want to laugh out loud. I might have skipped, if Tante Chouchotte hadn't been pulling me along, hurrying me toward my new, false life as a serious violinist. She would introduce me to Maître Crunelle in the morning, she said. She'd known him for years and he was the best. I was very lucky, and must work very hard. She hadn't realized I was so gifted, but if Henri said I was, I must be. My pension was on rue d'Assas, around the corner from her own apartment, and she knew the landlady, Madame Charpentier.

We passed through the gates of the Luxembourg, and the rain came all at once in great, cold drops. We ran down the path, past the flower beds and the fountain—rain streaming into my ears, between my shoulder blades—and then, as suddenly as it had begun, the torrent ceased. The sun broke through, glittering, washed, dripping off the trees and the gold-tipped gates. As if the city herself were welcoming me, showing herself off.

I stood in my new, small attic room, drenched to the bone, my stomach light and nervous. Cabbage-rose wallpaper covered the sloping ceiling and the low walls, as if I were in a garden. All warts and missing teeth, Madame Charpentier handed me the key and turned to leave. "Dinner is in half an hour," she said, over her shoulder. "If you're late, you won't be served. WC and bath down the hall, bathing privileges on Monday evening. No guests."

Tante Chouchotte kissed me good-bye then, instructing me to meet her the next evening at Simon and Michelle's. I must have looked surprised—Simon's wife was an idiot, and since their marriage, even my mother dreaded seeing him if it meant entertaining Michelle— but Tante Chouchotte whispered, "He has a radio." *I've only been in Paris an hour,* I thought, *and already I'm being trusted with secrets.*

I was dizzy with hunger, but I didn't want to go downstairs and meet the other boarders yet. I hardly knew what to say to girls my age, with their mysterious, laughing confidence, so I took off my wet clothes, climbed under the covers, and stared up through the skylight at the last blue of the evening. In the morning, when I opened my window, I disturbed a pair of doves. A sudden flapping of wings greeted me, a feathery applause.

· · ·

The pipes in the pension froze that winter—there was even less coal in Paris than in Caen, and for weeks we had no water at all, my toes were frostbitten, carbuncles appeared on the back of my neck—but the spring of '44 was so beautiful, with the chestnut trees blooming, the Luxembourg full of flowers. And the *boches* had left Italy! The Allies were bombing targets in Normandy and Cherbourg, and Maman had written that the weeds in the garden were getting thinned—she meant the *boches*. The *boches* were starting to move out of Caen.

I still had nightmares, but not as often, and there was another girl in the pension, Marie-Claire, from the Alps, who always smiled at me in the stairwell. The other tenants reminded me of Louis's old dancing partners—gossipy, kittenish girls who'd flirt with a *boche* for half a cigarette—but I liked Marie-Claire, with her rough clothes and mountain accent, a stack of books shoved under one arm.

And I liked Maître Crunelle. He had a long, grizzled face, like my father's, and he never let on that our lessons were pointless. He'd suggested that I learn Bach's Chaconne, a piece for which I had neither the skill nor the understanding, but I tried anyway. I would have added juggling to my audition if he'd asked.

At ten o'clock on the sixth of June, I presented

myself at the conservatory. I stood onstage, relaxed my shoulders, lifted my violin, my bow, and looked up—a window behind the assembled faculty made silhouettes of them all, and I couldn't make out their expressions. All I could see clearly was the bright, cloud-strewn Paris sky. A pigeon lifted off the windowsill, and I began.

My arms were suddenly leaden, my eyes stung. What had I been thinking? To try the Chaconne! To audition at all. I imagined Maître Crunelle, burning with shame on my behalf, and then I pictured Maman, with her hand raised, *Set yourself to the task before you!* But she had no idea how badly I played. She didn't know that Oncle Henri and I had tricked her. *You don't want to make a spectacle of yourself.*

I went straight to the pension when it was over and sat on the edge of the bed, as if I expected to hear from the conservatory any minute. The results would not be announced for weeks, but still, I didn't move. I might have sat there all night if I hadn't planned to meet Tante Chouchotte at Simon and Michelle's that evening.

Michelle opened the door, looked at me, and sighed. "I wish you hadn't come." She greeted me the same way every time, as if my being there increased the risk of being caught with a radio. "This is folly, pure folly. Your brother thinks nothing of the danger he's putting us in—of the danger to Xavier!"

Xavier, the baby, smiled placidly in his playpen. Despite her insistence that he was colicky, I'd never heard him cry, and their "small" apartment was, in fact, the entire floor of a building, lavishly appointed with Louis XIV chairs and Persian rugs.

Michelle sighed again, touching the ends of my hair. "You could be pretty if you tried, Geneviève. If you made a little effort." Simon was opening up the grandfather clock, pulling out the radio, and he glanced over at me apologetically. The same eyes as Louis, the same high forehead and narrow nose. The same thin mustache.

Tante Chouchotte had not yet arrived, and Michelle winked at me. "Why do you suppose your aunt is late?" she asked. "A lover, maybe? This is the third time this month. She's up to *something*. Some awful man in hiding, I imagine. A Jew, or a terrorist."

There was a familiar series of taps at the door, and Michelle bent over and fiddled with the baby. I opened the door for Tante Chouchotte and Michelle looked up, wide-eyed, as if she were surprised to see her. Michelle's shifts were impossible to make sense of. "Chouchotte," she said warmly, but Tante Chouchotte put her finger to her lips, and sat next to Simon. His face was white with expectation, the way it had been every evening for weeks now.

The radio crackled softly to life, the man from

Radio Libre began the personal announcements—coded messages for the Resistance—and stopped: "D-day has come!" he said. "D-day is here." The British and Americans were in Caen, they were all over the coast of Normandy.

"Oh!" Simon whispered. "Oh, God." And then we were all weeping and laughing, even Michelle. "Praise God," I said, and Tante Chouchotte shook her head, laughing, said God had nothing to do with it, the ones to thank were Churchill and Eisenhower. Michelle said, "I knew it, I felt it would be today," which was of course ridiculous, but no one minded. We could thank God, Michelle could say whatever came into her head, Simon could sit on the couch, chuckling, crying, and no one minded a thing. It was simply good to be together, to be alive in this world.

It was nearly curfew by the time we finished listening to the radio and had collected ourselves enough to think about heading home. "Stay," Michelle offered. "There's plenty of room." She made up beds for me and Tante Chouchotte and loaned us both nightgowns, as if all her gossip about Tante Chouchotte and her criticism of me had been nothing more than a passing fit.

In the morning, we went together to the town hall and the post office to see if there was any news from home. We knew it would take days for a message to reach us, but we couldn't help ourselves.

Though the *boches* were everywhere, patrolling the streets, I kept hearing Churchill's voice: he had come on the radio the night before to announce that the maneuvers had gone well, and casualties were limited. I imagined Maman going out into the street in Caen to greet the Allied soldiers. I wanted to ask her a thousand questions.

A week passed. Two. Every day, we went to the town hall and the post office, and every day, nothing. Lines of people like us waited for news, but the phones to the coast were down, the trains stopped. People arrived on foot and bicycle from Bayeux and Lisieux; they said there was fighting in the streets, and looting, that the bombs had not let up. All their news was old by the time they reached Paris.

I wasn't afraid. The *boches* had been heading out of Caen before D-day, so it wouldn't be too bad there. No, not fear—this was something different—a tension, an alertness.

By the third week, Tante Chouchotte had begun to snap at me, like my mother. Simon barely spoke to any of us anymore, and Michelle was herself again, restored. She burst into tears one day outside the post office. "What will become of them, Simon? Your mother, the little girls? Your *grandmother?* How will they manage? What if the Allies . . ." She lowered her voice: "What if they're not as *well behaved* as the Germans? Just think! A house full of women like that, with only one man to protect them!"

Her stupidity was like a circus trick, a thing barely to be believed.

"Simon!" Michelle insisted. "What will happen? With all those soldiers?" She was dismissive of Maman, paid no attention to my sisters or Grandmère, but her eyes brightened at the possibility of disaster. Of the Allies raping Yvonne and Françoise.

I didn't go back to my room, where my violin sat untouched. I couldn't stand those sloping walls anymore, with their riotous cabbage roses, or the noisy doves in the window. I went to the church of Saint-Étienne-du-Mont—into such darkness, silence. What light came through the stained-glass windows was the light of sunset, as if the day had collapsed into itself, and I was hours closer to seeing Maman. I could breathe. Time didn't stretch out painfully here, only to snap back like a rubber band against my heart, a sudden welt of fear. The church was still, quiet, holding its centuries of prayers and releasing them, a steady inhalation and exhalation of all human longing. Maman's prayers were here, too, I thought—the prayers of everyone who had ever lived—and I drank in the cool, dank air, as if I could draw Maman's faith into my own body.

The hospital in Caen would be overflowing with wounded soldiers; Maman would have taken

Yvonne and Françoise to volunteer with her, and the three of them would be washing linens, cleaning basins, bandaging wounds. All that blood, and neither Yvonne nor Françoise would utter a cry.

I slipped into a pew near the altar, knelt, and lay my head on my hands. *Dear God, please watch over the souls of Papa and Louis, please watch over Maman and Yvonne and Françoise, please watch over Tante Chouchotte, please help her to believe, and please watch over Simon and the baby. Please watch over all the dead and all the living, and help us to receive Your love, to know that we are blessed because You are with us*—but my prayers streamed over and around my actual thoughts: I wanted my mother to be thinking of me, to be *pleased* with me. I wanted someone—a boy, like Louis, who'd served in the cavalry—to slip into the pew beside me and shower me with praise. But for what? I was just tired. Hungry. I wanted chocolate more than anything. A boy with a bar of chocolate and a letter from Maman: *My darling Geneviève, I am so proud of you.* It was a sin to think of myself when the hospitals were full of wounded soldiers, but my ribs were sore, my belly small and tight. I wanted chocolate, a towering cake with chocolate ganache between the layers. *My wedding cake,* I thought, *when all of this is over.* Yes, a wedding! I'd wear a silk dress with tiny buttons down the back and a groom would feed me cake. A groom just like Louis. After the Battle of France, my groom would have escaped from a POW camp and joined the Maquis. I'd meet him here, where he'd have fled because—? He had typhoid fever. He'd been fighting the *boches*, he'd killed dozens of men, and now he was too sick. I would cool him with holy water, hold his head in my lap.

Forgive me my wickedness and my selfishness, forgive me my unbelief. But my groom thanked me over and over: I had saved his life, and I was so beautiful, in my dress with the tiny buttons.

It seemed as if I'd been kneeling for hours. It must be suppertime; I should go back to the pension and get a bowl of soup now. I would pray better tomorrow.

But when I pushed open the church doors, it was only midafternoon, the air hot and still. I paused on the church steps, and the sun-bleached flanks of the Panthéon burned my eyes. I didn't belong here. I pictured Maman before the war, feeding the chickens and the rabbits, weeding the garden. She'd come inside when she was done, her knees covered with dirt, and prepare our *goûter.* A square of dark chocolate tucked in a piece of bread. Useless thoughts. Better to take advantage of the sunshine and walk down to the river.

Without thinking, I crossed the Pont Royal and found myself in the Tuileries. I'd only been to the Tuileries once before. They were too close to the Forbidden Zone, *boches* marching up and down the broad, sandy avenues, singing their *val de ri, val de ra*; but today the gardens were deserted except for a few soldiers on patrol, a few old men reading *l'Action Française*, their white hair lifting in the breeze. I sat down on a bench and gave myself over to the afternoon heat until, suddenly, I was so relieved I burst out laughing: the family wasn't in Caen at all. Of course not! If the fighting and looting were as bad as people were saying, they would have gone to stay with Tante Alice in the countryside. She had chickens, vegetables, everything they needed. It was only a two-day walk to Tante Alice's. Three, maybe, with Grandmère in tow.

Even if it wasn't quite suppertime yet, I would ask for a bowl of soup. Because they were all safe, Maman, the little girls, everyone! I crossed the Pont Royal back toward the Left Bank, gazing down at the green, rippling water, at a pair of lovers resting against the railing, passing a cigarette back and forth. *A chocolate cake,* I thought, *a dress with tiny buttons down the back.*

On the far side of the river, a solitary, elegantly dressed man leaned over the railing, his head bobbing as if he were speaking to someone down below—it was Simon, in his blue suit, and he wasn't talking to anyone, he was weeping. I turned away, too embarrassed to walk past him. He might as well have been naked. Why was he here, on the Pont Royal, crying in the middle of the afternoon? What terrible thing had happened?

I glanced at him again—he seemed so thin, so broken—and then a pair of soldiers walked past him, laughing, and he pushed himself away from the railing. It wasn't Simon at all. The suit wasn't even the same shade of blue as his. I flushed, furious with myself. Of course they hadn't gone to Tante Alice's. Maman would never have left the wounded men. *Fear is a form of selfishness.*

The light over the city had grown thinner and softer, and when I entered the pension, I smelled the faint, bitter odor of turnips, but Madame Charpentier brushed me aside, said I'd wait for my soup like everyone else. This wasn't a restaurant, after all! I nodded, climbed the narrow, dusty stairs to my room, and there, on my bed, was a square white envelope addressed to me, and though it wasn't Maman's handwriting— it didn't belong to anyone I knew—my heart sped up, stabbing itself, and I couldn't open the envelope, my hands were too clumsy, the paper too thick and clean—

Chère Mademoiselle Delasalle,
I have the honor of informing you that your preliminary audition to the National Conservatory on the sixth of June, 1944, was successful—

My throat burned. If Maman really wanted to, she could have managed to send us a message. Other people had received letters, passed from one person to the next on the road to Paris, which was how we knew the bombing of the coast had not let up. But Maman was always late, always the last to show up. Any message from her would arrive after everyone else had gotten word.

I looked at Maître Crunelle's letter again and felt nothing, only a tiredness so deep I crawled under the covers with my clothes on.

When I awoke, I had missed supper. Carrot soup or turnip. Nothing to fill a stomach. It was almost curfew, too late to go to Simon and Michelle's to hear the radio. They would think I had gotten into trouble. Done something, gone somewhere we weren't allowed. I could just make it to Tante Chouchotte's in time to reassure her, but there was no way to get word to Simon. Simon, who was so gentle and quiet and never asked for anything.

Out on the street, everyone was hurrying to shelter, bicycles speeding through the fading light, *boches* on every corner. But Tante Chouchotte wasn't home. Madame Silva, the little Portuguese concierge, unlocked the door to Tante Chouchotte's room and shook her head mournfully. "I never know where your aunt spends the night."

I lay down on Tante Chouchotte's bed, gazing out over the piles of books and ashtrays; at her students' exams scattered on the floor beside the small round table where she ate and worked. The curtains were partly open, and a pale moon hung in the still-blue sky. I pulled the velvet coverlet up to my nose and breathed in the smell of Tante Chouchotte's cigarettes and men's cologne.

Would it have been such a sin, really, to marry Louis? I closed my eyes, gave myself over to the thought of a dress made of silk jacquard. Maman and I would sew it together. She would be the way she was at the beginning of the war, when I'd run to her bed at the sound of a siren. She used to lift the covers and slide over for me. Sleeping with me was like sleeping with a colt, she said: my spindly legs and hooves— my cold nose!—but she laughed when she said it, and pulled me into the warm crook of her arm.

I awoke to the sight of Tante Chouchotte looming over me and I sat up with a start: "Where were you?"

"Looking for you!" Tante Chouchotte pulled out her tobacco and rolling papers. "We were worried to death."

"Sorry—"

"Don't be an idiot," she said, softly, and she sat down beside me and stroked my forehead. Her hand was as large and strong as Maman's, but cooler, smelling of the night air, of cigarettes. "What happened to you?"

"I passed my audition. I thought the notice was a letter from Maman."

Tante Chouchotte gave a small, sad laugh but she didn't speak, her cigarette turning to ash. "Well," she said at last, "let's celebrate your success." She reached under her bed, scattering the ashes, pulled out a bag, and opened it. The smell of pepper and fat filled the room: at the bottom of the bag lay a *saucisson*. The end had been gnawed off, but it was a fat one, its powdery casing as white as the moon.

"Eat," Tante Chouchotte said, but I had already taken it. I was biting into the little pockets of fat, my face drenched with tears.

"There," said Tante Chouchotte, rolling herself a fresh cigarette, and then it came to me, sickeningly, that the *saucisson* might have been intended for Tante Chouchotte's lover. I stopped eating. "Was this—?" I began. "Did you mean this for someone else?"

Tante Chouchotte's eyes widened. "No," she said. "What an idea! I got it for later, for"—she laughed—"an emergency. If things get even worse. But the rats keep getting into it." She stared at me for a moment. "Whatever I've done— whoever I've helped and wherever I found this— it isn't something to discuss, do you understand?"

I blushed, and then I took another bite. The fat

coated my teeth, and suddenly I felt that I had never been happier; I held the *saucisson* out for Tante Chouchotte. When we had eaten almost all of it, Tante Chouchotte smiled, flashing her gold tooth. "Let's go to bed. We can finish this little bit in the morning. I promised Simon I'd find you and meet up with him early. He'll be pleased about your audition."

Tante Chouchotte lay close behind me, the smell of *saucisson* on our hands, our breath, the sheets, as if the war were already over, and we could eat freely for the rest of our lives.

We overslept and when we awoke, Tante Chouchotte jumped out of bed and handed me my clothes. No time to wash up or use the toilet, she said. Simon would be sick with worry if we were late.

It was beautiful outdoors, the sky above the tall, lovely buildings like blue silk, a breeze blowing in off the Atlantic, flattening women's skirts against their legs, and ruffling the fur of a poodle relieving himself in the Luxembourg. I was still full from the night before, and if I softened my gaze, I could imagine, as we hurried toward rue Soufflot, that the patisserie was full of bread and croissants, that they were serving real coffee at Le Rostand, but just then Simon and Michelle appeared, running toward us.

Michelle had the exalted look of someone who, for once, has been proven right. "Your mother's dead," she called out, her eyes feverish. "Your mother, your grandmother, the darling Yvonne. A bomb fell on your house. Only your stepfather and Françoise survived!"

Before the words could sort themselves in my mind, my stomach dissolved, my bones turned to water. *Maman is dead, Maman, Yvonne, Grandmère.* I felt the warmth of my bladder emptying onto the sidewalk, the breezy warmth of the summer day.

Years later, when we were already very old, and hardly anyone alive even remembered the war, Simon told me that Tante Chouchotte stood on the sidewalk screaming. He'd never heard a scream like that before.

"That's all you remember?" I asked. "Nothing else?"

"I knew then I'd have to divorce Michelle."

"But nothing else from that day? You don't remember me?"

"You didn't show up—we were all so worried."

"But I *was* there."

"No, it was just Chouchotte, screaming."

I couldn't imagine Chouchotte screaming— Chouchotte, who had long ceased to be the chain-smoking aunt of my youth and who had become, in the end, simply an old woman, fat and gossipy, with a bag of candy in her pocket for the little children.

But I remembered the sensation of peeing in front of everyone. I hadn't been embarrassed, I hadn't been able to see anyone clearly enough to be embarrassed; the sky had darkened, and nothing held together. The knowledge of my mother's death kept coming at me, over and over, but I didn't faint, I held my head up to the dark, shattering sky and raised my arms, "Lord, they are with you!" Someone slapped me, I stumbled back on the pavement, and then I could see again: Simon in his brown suit and Michelle with her little pink hat, the patisserie with its empty shelves, and next to it, the café where all the customers sat motionless, watching us.

I saw everything: the bright, blue, silken sky; the trembling leaves of the plane trees; the dappled shadows on the sidewalk almost camouflaging the splash of urine between my feet; and Chouchotte, with her hand still raised, as if she meant to slap me again. "Don't you dare bring God into this."

And although Chouchotte apologized to me later, and everyone was very kind, what I would carry with me for the rest of my life was the feel of Chouchotte's palm against my cheekbone, the hard, flat sting of it, like my mother's.

THE MOTHER

There are guards in front of Raphaël's house, swastikas hanging from his windows. The sight knocks the wind out of me and I stop like a fool in the middle of the street. A bicycle weaves past me, and Madame Fleury, walking back from the square, wishes me good morning, but I can't stop looking at the house. Black-and-red banners fluttering against the stone. If one of my girls behaved this way, I'd slap her, tell her to get hold of herself—I need to get to the butcher's, see if he has anything besides horse marrow today— but I don't move.

The street rises toward me, as if I might faint, but the moment passes. Why should the swastikas on Raphaël's house make me dizzy? There are swastikas all over town. My son Louis was killed in the Battle of France two years ago and I didn't faint then. I didn't faint when half the city fled, their belongings piled into wheelbarrows and baby carriages, or when Huntziger signed the surrender and gave everything to the Germans. I learned to turn rabbits into coats and stews, make bread from cornmeal and molasses, stretch out a turnip soup to last the week. I taught the children I still had not to cry.

But now, when there's a whole day's shopping still ahead of me—the lines, the jostling, the possibility, if I hurry, of getting something better than horse marrow, a bit of liver, maybe—I can't move. The guards could shoot the pavement, scare me off like a stray dog, but they won't. I'm not worth the trouble, a middle-aged housewife listing before them in the breeze.

I imagine the officers inside: a dozen of them, sitting down to breakfast. Croissants so warm and tender that even the officers are moved to tears, the finest coffee, and for each man, his own bowl of sugar. But what difference does any of that make? What difference if, even now, some lieutenant is bathing in Raphaël's bathtub and another one is spitting in his sink? If a third, washed and fed, is sitting idly at the piano, running his fingers over the keys?

What matters is that Raphaël is gone, that he escaped just in time and the rumor is that they're still looking for him, which means they haven't found him, which means he's safe. And though it's sickening to see Germans living in his house, the only surprise is that they did not requisition it long ago. They let him stay there—a Jew!—and didn't move in until he left.

For two years, we begged him to go. He shrugged us off, he even grinned. He wasn't a practicing Jew, he said, he was a Frenchman, as if that made a difference. He knew it didn't—he'd sent his wife south right after the surrender—but even after they stripped him of his license, forced him to pin a star to his jacket, he didn't follow her. He stayed in Caen, for the ocean breeze, he insisted. And if a child was sick, he went discreetly to the patient's house. He had no medicine, but he could diagnose a rash, set a dislocated limb, apply a poultice. He kept laughing as if nothing had changed, performing his card and coin tricks to distract the children from their pain.

"The man's a fool," my mother said, and then, as if she knew everything: "Like you, Pauline."

But Raphaël did leave, finally. Two weeks ago, his parents were arrested and he was gone the next day. God keep him safe.

Beneath the ruffling banners, the guards stand perfectly still, indifferent to my gawking. I taste something metallic, like a storm, but the air is light today, the sky clear.

I've never told anyone about Raphaël, not even the priest. I have other sins to reveal in the confessional, and I wouldn't know what to say about Raphaël. It was all such a long time ago! Almost twenty years. We were still reeling from the last war, could not have dreamed up this one. I was a newlywed still, simpleminded as a child, and I suppose my innocence was the start of everything. When I'd told my mother I was marrying Daniel Delasalle, she burst into tears. "A diabetic!" she cried. "You'll be a widow before you're twenty-five."

"I don't care," I said. "I would die for him." Daniel seemed so strong to me. He was a handsome man—broad shoulders; thick, wild eyebrows—but I can't remember if his eyes were hazel or brown.

Within a year, Daniel himself suggested an annulment. We were nineteen and twenty and we spent our days laughing, making up pet names for each other, who knows what. He said our marriage hadn't been properly consummated, that he might never be able to be a true husband. I had no idea what he was talking about. We clung to each other every night and he touched me in places I did not know the names of. Not a stitch of clothing between us. It was something I could not permit myself to think of for more than a minute or two in the light of day. How could I have known a marriage required anything else? The nuns had taught me to change my clothes and bathe without fully undressing and, until my wedding night, I'd never seen myself naked.

"We may never be able to have children," he went on.

I'd been heating the milk for his coffee and I turned the stove off so sharply the knob fell into my hand. "Stop it," I said and I went to sit on his lap. I breathed in the sweet, diabetic smell of him, a smell I loved beyond all reason. "You're all I need."

He wasn't, of course. A few months later, Raphaël—he was still Docteur Naquet to me then—mentioned a pair of four-year-old twin orphans in need of a home. I can't remember why we were talking, or even where we ran into each other. I took Raphaël's hand in mine though I barely knew him and said I'd take the twins. *Simon and Louis.* Raphaël laughed, that easy laugh of his, as if the whole world were a delightful joke. "Your husband will agree, Madame?"

"He'll be so happy," I said, imagining him reading to them at night while I darned socks.

"Very well, then, Madame." Raphaël laughed again. "The boys will be happy, too."

I can see his eyes perfectly: round and blue as a robin's eggs. He's a short, plump man, but all the mothers adored him.

When Simon came down with polio, Raphaël drove him to the hospital—Daniel was at work—and afterward, he came back to the house, where I was waiting with Louis on my lap, afraid to let him out of my sight. Raphaël patted my hand. "It's an excellent hospital, Madame, and we've caught it early." And then, because Louis kept squirming, he pretended to find a coin behind Louis's ear. "Again!" Louis begged, and Raphaël produced coin after magical coin.

Four and a half months later, when Simon was discharged with nothing more than a limp, the hospital said it was Raphaël's early diagnosis that had saved Simon's life. I made an apple cake to celebrate his homecoming, though I didn't often make desserts, since Daniel couldn't eat them.

We stood together on the terrace after we'd put the boys to bed, taking in the evening air. "You should bake something for the doctor," Daniel said.

A breeze lifted toward us, carrying with it the smell of honeysuckle. Or maybe I was just smelling Daniel.

"Oh," I said. "I don't want to be like the other mothers. You have no idea, Daniel. They give the doctor little presents all the time, wear their best dresses when they go to see him."

"One cake," he said. "That's perfectly respectable."

And so I took Raphaël and his wife a cake. It was a delicate little almond cake, warm from the oven, but then, because Simon was sick again that fall, I took over some profiteroles. When Louis broke his arm, I made a tarte tatin, the apples perfectly caramelized. Later—I can't remember the occasion—an opera cake. Once I had started baking, it seemed, I couldn't stop.

All that time alone in the kitchen was too much. A girl ought to avoid daydreams. I'd figured out by then how our marriage was unusual, though I never worried about Daniel's health. I could no more imagine his mortality than my own, but the lives of children seemed so fragile, like seedlings loose in the ground. It was Simon who could have died!

Louis tore up the garden with his games—Simon, still weak, leaned against the apple tree, laughing—and all that time, while I was beating egg whites, melting chocolate, grinding nuts, I thought of nothing but babies, as if a dozen children could protect me from the loss of any one. Not just any babies: my own. The warmth of a newborn in my arms, my body sufficient for its needs. A pleasure I'd never know, I thought.

You're spoiling us, Raphaël's wife said, each time I showed up with dessert.

Oh, I'd say. *We had extra. We are so grateful to your husband.*

An extra tarte tatin? Whoever heard of such a thing? I made a fool of myself like all the other mothers, but Raphaël's wife barely let on. There was only the briefest flash of irritation in her eyes. She was a tall woman, very striking, with hair as black as an Oriental's and beautiful posture. She would accept my gift at the front door without inviting me in, and I'd smile at her a little too eagerly. I never saw Raphaël when I brought him gifts, but I could hear him in the back of the house, playing the piano, and I strained to listen.

I have no ear, so it wasn't the music that moved me, but the fact of his playing after a long day of soothing brows and taking temperatures.

Sometime around the opera cake, or maybe it was when I took over a chocolate torte, his wife didn't answer the door. The housemaid appeared, Mathilde, so delicate and blond I could not help gaping at her. "Madame is out of town," she said and she ushered me in as if I were an important guest. She went to the back of the house and the piano stopped abruptly. Raphaël came out with his bag already in hand, saw me, and asked if everyone was all right. "Oh, yes," I said. I had just brought him a little something. He smiled at Mathilde, nodding as if to say it's all right, you can go, but in the future, I'm only to be disturbed if a child is sick. Mathilde blushed, the color rising from her collarbone to her crown, and I handed her the dessert, marveling at her nearly transparent skin. I had a flash of jealousy, some annoyance that all the women in the Naquet household were so beautiful, and I was about to leave when Raphaël sighed suddenly. "Come in, Madame Delasalle," he said, and helped me out of my coat.

He led me down the hall, into the room with the piano, and we sat facing each other, not saying a word. For once, his eyes weren't full of laughter and I was so uncomfortable I could not stop jiggling my knee. He asked after the family, finally, and I said everyone was well and that I was terribly sorry to disturb him. He smiled a little and lit a cigarette. "Nonsense, Madame Delasalle. I'm happy to be disturbed, as you say. My wife has gone to visit her relatives in Nantes and it's nice to have a bit of company."

His father-in-law was very ill, he said, and I murmured my condolences. Then I asked him what he'd been playing on the piano, as if it would mean anything to me.

"I'm sorry," he said. "I'm being a poor host. The truth is—if you wouldn't mind—may I finish the piece I was practicing? Then we can have a proper visit."

"Please," I said. "Continue. I'd love to hear you." I couldn't offer to leave again, and force him to reassure me once more that I wasn't a disturbance. I folded my hands on my lap, pressing down on my restless knee.

He smiled at me, and then he went to the piano, lifted his hands, and began to play. His mouth fell open, twisting the way a musician's mouth will do, revealing that depth of concentration which always riveted me more than any actual piece of music. His eyebrows arched, fell, and his head tilted from side to side. He seemed almost naked, and though I felt that I should look away, I couldn't. He always looked at *others,* peering into throats and ears, examining backs, chests, the soles of feet, and his sudden exposure burned my eyes, made my heart leap in my throat. Even then, I didn't understand the true nature of my feelings. He stopped suddenly, closed the lid of the piano, and rose, his face relaxed again and his eyes once more amused, as if I shouldn't take anything—not even his music—too seriously.

"You're very kind," he smiled, mistaking my obvious emotion for an appreciation of the music.

"That was wonderful," I said, glancing down at my hands. My fingernails were still dirty from planting daffodils earlier.

"I didn't know you were a music lover."

"Yes," I murmured, embarrassed by my own act. My pretense of sophistication!

"Well," he said brightly, "let's taste this lovely thing you've brought me."

"Oh, *Docteur*," I said. "I couldn't. It's for you."

He laughed, patting his sturdy stomach. "With my wife gone, I'm in danger of eating the whole thing. Please, help me." He laughed again: "I'm the beneficiary of far too many pastries, you know. And though I'm usually able to show some restraint, you seem to be the best patissier in Caen, Madame."

I flushed, thinking of Daniel, who could eat none of my pastries.

"Surely you're not worried about your figure?"

I shook my head.

"A glass of port, then? You won't refuse me that, will you, after all your kindness?"

"It's you who are kind, *Docteur*."

"Come," he laughed. "Let's taste this."

I accepted the port then, relieved that I'd gone to his house in a plain housedress, though I couldn't have known I'd see him. Still, it seemed like a mark of virtue.

But the glass trembled in my hand and I had trouble forming words. He kept smiling at me, always on the point of laughter, as if I and my simple dress and the dessert I'd brought and the port we were drinking were the loveliest things he could imagine.

I finished my glass too quickly and when I got up to leave, I wobbled a little. I wasn't used to drinking anything strong. He caught me by the elbow. "Madame Delasalle," he said. "Pauline." He'd never used my first name before, and for an instant I bristled, thinking he saw me as one of his patients. A child.

"Docteur Naquet," I said.

"Please, call me Raphaël."

"I should—" I said, but I couldn't say what it was I should do. My hands were shaking.

He urged me to sit down again, but I kept standing.

"Shall I see you home?" he asked, finally.

I looked away.

He laughed a little. "I'm not sure if that's a yes or a no."

I put my fingers to his lips. They were very full, and soft, like a woman's.

Afterward, I walked home alone. He called a taxi for me, but I got out as soon as it had turned the corner. It was misting out, and I remember the silence of the streets, the dark, slick cobblestones. I could have walked forever, down to the river and out to the edge of town, all the way to the ocean.

Daniel was waiting for me in his bathrobe, reading the paper. I'd outstripped him, I thought, and that was the worst of it. I'd done what he couldn't do. As if, with every kiss of Raphaël's, I'd told Daniel, *You'll die. I'll live on for years, do things you cannot dream of.* It was the first time I believed I might lose him.

Daniel knew what had happened, of course, what can happen so easily between a healthy young woman and a healthy man. I'd been gone over three hours. He said nothing, but I could see it in his face—a tension I'd never noticed in his features was gone, as if he'd been expecting this, waiting for it. He put down his paper, came to me, and held me for a long time. We went to bed without a word and I clung to him all night, alert with something I couldn't name.

In the morning, when he could see that I'd barely slept, that my eyes were red, he sat me down and said, very sternly—it was the only time I ever saw him angry and it cauterized something in me—"Don't ever pity me, Pauline. I am the happiest of men."

It was only the one time with Raphaël. His father-in-law died and his wife was gone for a long time, but I did not go to check on him, not even to bring him some of the apples from our tree, though we had more than we could eat that year, more than I could even turn into applesauce. Sometime after his wife came back, she fired their maid and the last time anyone saw Mathilde, she was at the station, boarding the train for Paris, as lovely as ever with her silky hair and her porcelain skin, but noticeably plumper, everyone agreed.

I was visibly pregnant myself by then, the child in my womb so restless I thought the whole town could see its turning and kicking. My body seemed to double in size, my face growing so round I could have been a Naquet myself. I loved the feel of the baby swimming inside my body, but, God forgive me, I was glad about Mathilde. Glad at the expense of that poor, ruined girl, because the scandal kept all eyes off me.

Not that anyone suspected what I'd done. No one besides Daniel and Raphaël had reason to make assumptions, especially since all the mothers blushed at the sight of Raphaël. I was just the one who had appeared when his wife was out of town, before Mathilde had learned that she should not disturb the good doctor except for a medical emergency, that she was company enough in his wife's absence.

All through my pregnancy, I dreamed of Raphaël. When I awoke from those dreams, my skin was sore and it was hard to swallow anything, but Daniel treated all my symptoms as morning sickness. I mustn't tire myself, he said. I was giving him the greatest possible gift. The two of us were more tender with each other than we'd ever been.

I never took Raphaël another dessert, not even after he took care of Simon when he had the measles or fixed Louis's broken arm or, miraculously, cured Geneviève of her colic. He did not treat Geneviève any differently from the other children, although once he said she was a beautiful baby in a way that was different from the way he complimented most children. I gave him a thin, disapproving smile, as if I had no idea why he'd talk to me that way. As if I never thought of him when I was alone, remembering the practiced feel of his hands.

Once, a few years later, I overheard Daniel talking to him. Raphaël had come to see Louis, who had tonsillitis, and I stayed back with Louis for a few minutes after Raphaël went downstairs. When I followed him a few minutes later to settle the bill, I found him in the living room with Daniel and Geneviève. She was kneeling on the carpet, talking to her dolls, and Raphaël and Daniel were standing side by side, watching her, chuckling. She started to sing a little song she'd learned—she was two or three and the words were all mixed up—and Daniel, nearly a head taller than Raphaël, put his hand on Raphaël's shoulder. "She doesn't miss a note, *Docteur*. She has your ear."

After Daniel died, I married Henri Manier. That was ten years ago. Henri had known Daniel when they were boys, and he was very helpful those last years, when Daniel was confined to his sickbed. Henri is the most resourceful man I know, and I couldn't have managed without him. I'd given birth to two more daughters by the time I buried Daniel, and though it must be obvious to everyone that Henri is Yvonne's and Françoise's father—they look exactly like him, and he's more attentive toward them than the others—no one would guess about Geneviève. Only her eyes are Raphaël's.

And yet Daniel was my true love, the boy I grew up with. I was thirteen when we met, a girl still playing a child's games. He carved a doll for me once, from a bit of wood. Sometimes I dream he's alive, and it's just the two of us, alone in the world. I'm so happy to be with him, and then I begin to notice the others—Henri,

Raphaël, the children—and the dream splinters off in a thousand directions. I forget Daniel altogether, until the middle of the next day, when the beginning of the dream comes back to me, an ache in my sternum.

But other days, it's Raphaël's company I crave. Not to make love with, just to sit beside me, talk to me about Geneviève. To remind me that, although Daniel is dead, she still has a father. Henri is a good man, but he doesn't love Geneviève or the boys the way Daniel loved all our children.

The guards haven't moved. If they've noticed me, staring up at them, they don't show it. *Be safe, Docteur*, I think, snapping out of it, finally, and I turn away from Raphaël's house, and head toward the square.

There's a line down the street at the butcher's, and I stand with everyone else in the bright sunshine, waiting my turn for a bit of horse marrow to last the week, thinking I'll go ahead and cook up the old rabbit I've been saving, too. Madame Vilnier asks after the children and I smile at her. "They're fine," and then, not to be outdone in small talk, I say what a nice day it is, I'll be happy if the good weather keeps up. I shake my head in dismay when Madame Grouls says there isn't even any cornmeal left at the grocer's and again when Madame Marcher says her son-in-law has been called up to work in Germany.

And then I take my horse marrow home, where Louis's horse tack is still hanging inside the back door, and there's a letter from Simon on the kitchen table—he lives in Paris now, spared from combat by his limp. Yvonne is lying on the sofa, planning mischief, no doubt; my littlest, Françoise—so much more dutiful than her siblings!—is scrubbing the front hall; and Geneviève is shut up in her room, playing the violin. She shouldn't spend so much time by herself, it isn't healthy. I make my way upstairs to look in at her, with her blue, blue eyes, her face distorted like all great musicians' faces, though Henri says she isn't very good, and what would I know? I was going to tell her to come downstairs and help me with the supper, but she's so lovely, standing there, not even aware of me, the bow of her violin coming down and down and down.

MATHILDE

I am old enough that people congratulate me on the simple fact of being alive—*Marie-Claire, they say, you're astonishing*—but until I was this old I always thought, *Please, God, not me.* Please let me die before I've lost my senses and no one wants to listen to me anymore. My children pause, *We know, Maman, you've told us that already.* Five sons, all so mysterious to me. When they wheel me out to take the air, they watch for my last breath and I can't tell if they're afraid of what's to come or, poor souls, just tired of waiting.

I always loved heights, could hardly keep myself from jumping just for the thrill of it, but now it's as if I stood on the far edge of the world, hesitating. There are still things I want to say, even if I have already said them. Judgments I'd like to retract. What I thought of Mathilde Antonna, for example.

I was seventeen when Mathilde and her son, Marcel, came to us, and I believed her claim, circulated throughout the village, that she was a widow. Why would she lie? No one, I thought, not even a divorced woman, would invent a dead husband. My own mother was divorced and she bore her shame bravely.

The women in the village whispered among themselves that Mathilde Antonna was a girl-mother. That much was obvious, they said; the only question was why she had come to us: Why not go to the seaside? It's a hard life in the mountains, with snow half the year and so little room to grow anything.

The women took their gossip with them, trailing it from store to store, and I trailed along behind. Mathilde, they insisted, was too pretty. She couldn't be much past—what? Thirty? And the boy was surely sixteen.

The expression itself—"girlmother"—made no sense to me. I didn't know it was possible to conceive a child outside of marriage. Despite all I'd seen of cows and dogs and cats and goats, I didn't realize humans went about things in the same way. I heard "girlmother" and pictured a child playing house. But I knew that wasn't right; it was clear the village women meant something monstrous and, because Mathilde's sin was connected to her beauty, I thought my ugliness must be a virtue. Of course I wasn't truly ugly— the young are beautiful, no matter what—but I was poor, tall as a boy, and bony.

Mathilde and Marcel arrived in the fall, when the leaves here turn so fast a fire seems to rage throughout the valley, though the wind is damp and raw. I remember that I heard about them on a Sunday. On Sundays, I went to the boulangerie and the butcher's so that my mother would be spared the embarrassment of coming from a different direction than everyone else. The embarrassment of not making her way down the steps of the church with the rest of the village and crossing the square with two or three other women to the stores on the other side. I didn't go to church either, but I hadn't been excommunicated. I avoided church out of loyalty to my mother and also because, though I believe in God, the idea of a father orchestrating his son's crucifixion strikes me as the stuff of nightmares. Abraham and Isaac, God and Jesus—I never liked those stories.

A Sunday, then, and I was doing the shopping. From the store side of the square, you can see Mont Blanc, rising up behind the church. It has nothing to do with my story, but how to speak of my village without naming the mountains all around? *Mont Blanc, the Aiguilles, the Grandes Jorasses, Mont Maudit, Mont Blanc du Tacul.* The sky was the deep, rich, icy blue you only see in the Alps, and the racks and bins at the boulangerie were still full of bread, the smell of yeast so tantalizing it seemed almost visible, as if it hung suspended in the midday light. This was 1939, when we still had plenty of food.

The Widow Charles, who was half blind, announced to the store at large that Mathilde's gait said it all, and the others murmured in agreement, a gentle, fascist chorus. Nicole Lagrange, the mayor's wife, leaned toward the Widow Charles, shaping the air with her slender fingers. She seemed to cup the words—"girl" "mother"—in her hands, as if she meant to fling them outside onto the cobblestones.

Ever since my mother had found a decorated hairpin in the pocket of my father's coat and demanded that he leave, she and I had been the lowest of the low; in those days, a wife was supposed to tolerate a bit of infidelity. I was eight at the time, and I thought my mother was simply angry that my father had forgotten to empty his pockets—she was a meticulous woman—but in the years since, waiting in one line or another, I'd overheard enough to piece together the truth: my father was living with a woman in Annecy. My mother, the village women said, had done nothing to make herself appealing, as if her plainness were the crime, so I was only mildly curious about Mathilde and Marcel now; what fascinated me was this new connection between homeliness and salvation. I gazed down happily at my big, chapped hands, my worn boots, and stopped trying to make sense of what a "girlmother" was or how a person could be a round bread, which was the only meaning I knew for *bâtard*.

But the very next day Marcel appeared on the train to school, and, however beautiful his mother might be, he reminded me of a giraffe, with his long neck and thin, freckled forehead.

We took the train to school only if the weather was too bad for bikes or skis—if it was sleeting, or the wind was especially strong, or the fog too heavy. All of us from the surrounding villages would take over a single coach, though once we reached Chamonix, of course, the boys went one way and the girls went another. While the others laughed and told stories, I read fitfully, distracted by the rain and the wind, and the sensation I love so much of being suspended above the gorges. Because of the bad weather, I couldn't see how precipitously the earth fell away, first on one side, then another, as the train wound along its tracks, but I felt it. I imagined the railcars tumbling out into nothingness and the thought of so much space thrilled me.

The older students—the ones in my grade—sat on one side of the railcar and the little ones sat on the other, but I took a bench by myself, near the door. Marcel stood not far from me, holding on to a strap and swaying with the train's movement. I could tell he wasn't used to the mountains, the way he lost his balance every time the train went around a curve—he wasn't used to the winding, or the sheets of rain, or the black cliffs appearing suddenly in the windows, and I wondered if he was glancing at me as I glanced at him. I blushed, embarrassed, and suddenly I understood that we belonged together, with our lonely mothers and our clumsy bodies. Ugliness wasn't, after all, a virtue. I could see my own raw, knobby knees swimming in my peripheral vision, and his boots and the bottoms of his trousers. The fabric was too thin; those trousers wouldn't do him any good once winter came, and his boots, though adequate, looked as if they'd never been worn before. I gazed up the length of his leg, forgetting my embarrassment. I tended to swing between imagining that everyone was talking about me and imagining that I didn't exist, and in my nonexistent moments, I'd developed a bad habit of staring. Since I stayed away from my peers and wore thick glasses, people rarely noticed, but Marcel stood maybe a meter from where I sat.

When I reached his crotch—which, after all, was right at eye level—the blood seemed to drain out of me. If I had failed to understand that humans procreate the way animals do, it's because it had never occurred to me that our genitals were so like theirs. I'd never given any thought to the workings of a boy's body, but now, with Marcel so close, I pictured all those bulls and dogs and cats and goats I'd seen, and I understood that being smooth-skinned and walking on two legs changed nothing.

It's hard to believe I'd been so obtuse until that moment, but when I consider my life, it's all one long story of obtuseness. In any case, gazing straight at Marcel's crotch clarified a great deal for me: what a girlmother was, a bastard, even the full extent of my father's offense. And though at first I felt sick, as if the ground had opened up beneath me, I was also thrilled: the ground had opened up beneath me.

My mother never spoke of the way she was treated, but she never spoke much at all. When she confronted my father with the hairpin, she set it on the kitchen table instead of the bowl of soup he was expecting, and returned to the stove to ladle out my dinner. More discussion would have struck her as ridiculous as the hairpin itself. She was so averse to waste of any kind—of words, time, money—that even the slenderness of her bones seemed a measure of her thrift.

I could have told anyone who'd care to listen how sad she was. When Nicole Lagrange and the other women looked away from me or her, or made it clear that they were talking about us— even if my mother was safely at home, bent over the fine-stitch sewing that earned our keep—I felt the tightness in my mother's ribs, her echoing loneliness, and I couldn't swallow.

She wanted me to go to Paris someday, to study at Sèvres and become a teacher, and, while I studied, she took in sewing and did the housework. The other children in the village milked and herded cows, cleaned stalls, cut hay, split wood, and shoveled snow, but I sat and read while my mother scrubbed our floors and windows, washed our laundry, fed our fire, made our supper; while she sewed baptismal and communion and wedding gowns that were famous in six villages for the precision of their stitching, their fine and elaborate pleats and smocking and tucks and gathers. Her stitches, our house, her soul—everything she tended to was flawless.

Except for me. I overspilled my bounds, wanting the world. I didn't want to be a girlmother, but I wanted Marcel for my own. Once I understood the possibilities, I couldn't think of anything else. It could have been anyone, but Marcel was the only option I could see— what did I care that he was a bastard?

That evening, while my mother said her prayers—despite everything, she still believed in Jesus and Mary and all the rest—I tried to picture Marcel without his clothes, and, as Jesus was the only notion I had of a naked man, that's how I saw him, wounds and all, a cloth across his lap, his arms wide open.

The first time I saw Mathilde, I was near enough to touch her, and I almost did. It was another Sunday, and I had stepped into the boulangerie for a baguette. Before the fog of my glasses evaporated, I was startled by the silence—no one was talking at all, as if some awful thing had just happened—and then my glasses cleared, and I saw her, saw the little space around her the others had left while they carried out their wordless transactions. It wasn't as if the usual banter had ever been necessary—the boulanger already knew what each woman wanted—but Mathilde didn't understand the patois we spoke amongst ourselves. Their silence was just as unnecessary. She was last in line, and I took my place behind her, my heart beating so fast I imagined she could feel its vibration. By now I had seen Marcel several times, and though we had never looked at each other directly, I was more and more sure of our bond. Here was his mother—and by extension, I felt, mine, as if we were already in-laws. She was looking down, studying the prepared dishes, so that I could see her profile. It wasn't her white-blond hair or her translucent skin that struck me first, the way they had everyone else; it was her meekness. Shoulders bowed, her hair fixed in a small bun, she looked like a girl called up before the Mother Superior. I stared at the faint down on the curve of her neck, her simple white collar, the gold cross dangling from her throat—she had clearly been to mass with the others—and I knew she was innocent of all the accusations made against her. She was no more capable of sin than my own mother.

I wanted to go up to each woman in line and tell her how wrong she'd been: Nicole Lagrange, the Widow Charles, fat old Madame Carreaux, and jolly Madame Désailloux with her two jolly married daughters. I would have liked to grab them by the hair and slap them for all the times they'd whispered about my mother, stared at her, glanced at the two of us with their false smiles. I may have been a quiet girl, but I had a good imagination. I saw myself knocking their heads together, pair by pair, and then taking Mathilde's hand and running away with her. I'd take her down to the stream I liked to go to when the weather was nice and we'd sit on the flat rock beneath the poplars, the water parting around us. I'd brush out her hair.

She was gazing down at the prepared dishes—the greasy rillettes and the smooth pâté, the speckled quiche and the golden flan—as if she were afraid to speak. Then, suddenly, she was placing her order, her voice breaking into the silence not like the soprano flute I expected from such delicate features, but like a cello, deep and almost painful. *One baguette and two pieces of flan, please.*

After she had paid, when she turned to leave, I smiled at her—I who never smiled at anyone. She smiled back, her teeth as small and even as a child's, and hesitated for a moment, as if we should speak, but of course we didn't. Still, there was that startled smile, the pause, and after that I smiled whenever I saw her and she smiled back, a smile so warm it was as if we knew each other's secrets. I thought she knew how lonely I'd been and that I didn't judge her, and I believed she loved me.

Winter came, and there was talk of the boys going to the front, but none of them had yet, and the war still seemed far away. Or maybe it's only now, knowing what came later, that the early days of the war seem so harmless. What I remember is how the world felt new to me, the snow itself like a thing I'd never witnessed: the flakes melting on my tongue, and the deepening drifts, the ache of the wind—an ache inseparable from my own desire, but whether that desire was for Mathilde or Marcel, I hardly knew, could hardly tell them apart, the one so small and good, the other so gangly and solemn. I wanted Marcel to touch me and I wanted Mathilde to ask after me.

On Sundays, when they walked past our chalet to mass, he towered over her, his head bent toward hers as if he were confiding in her, but it was just bad posture. He barely spoke to his mother any more than he spoke to anyone else.

The only real similarity between them was how pale they were, and I came to see their complexion—his especially, with all its freckles—as a sign of vulnerability, the flush of his cheeks evidence of his perpetual morti-fication. He must know what people said about him and his mother, how they discounted the existence of his father. What could he do but look away?

Mathilde wouldn't know. Surely she wouldn't be able to fathom what everyone else was imagining, and that was why she was so much lovelier than Marcel. She was no more capable of gossip than she was of sin.

But Marcel! The more he wanted to express—even feelings of love, of kindness—the more withdrawn he grew. This was how I explained the fact that he had not once glanced in my direction. Of course, he looked at no one, but I was sure he avoided me most of all.

I prayed for bad weather so that we could ride the train, so that I could watch him as he leaned skillfully now into the curves, could see his Adam's apple jump as the space below us came into view—as I myself swallowed, imagining the rush of air. No one else on the train even seemed to notice the drop.

I pictured going to church with him and Mathilde, sitting beside him and feeling the fabric of his trousers against my knee. I would have gone—I would have put aside my horror of the crucifixion to sit beside them—but I didn't want to hurt my mother.

I can't explain what it was like to be young in those days, how heady it all was, with the war spreading across Europe, and desire all tangled up with death. I was thrilled that cold spring morning in 1940, when our boys went off to fight. The sky was crystal blue, fog drifted across the valley, and Mont Blanc rose in the distance like the entrance to Paradise. Across from the snow-covered massif, the Aiguilles glistened blackly.

Marcel slumped against the station wall in an overcoat whose sleeves were too short, staring at the ground. I stood a little ways from him, behind a post, daring myself to go up to him, to throw my arms around his neck and kiss his cheeks. Everyone was crying and kissing—who would even notice my display? I imagined Marcel blushing, stammering maybe. He'd have to look at me. My father, whose eyes I inherited, sometimes said how pretty mine were when he still lived with us. Marcel would gaze into them and put his arms around me. I touched my mouth: he'd press his red, chapped lips against mine.

Mathilde wept, like all the mothers, but she wasn't clinging to her son the way they were, and she seemed more out of place than she'd ever seemed at the boulangerie or in the square. She'd come down to the station without a coat—all she wore with her dress was an old cardigan and boots—and her arms hung helplessly at her sides. She looked even younger than the village women claimed, and it seemed she barely knew Marcel. It seemed as if she wept for no reason.

My heart was racing. *They don't know what to do with themselves,* I thought, *how to be a family.* If I went up to Marcel, if I touched him, Mathilde would smile through her tears, so grateful for my presence in their lives. I held on to the post, giddy and shivering. We would only have a few minutes together before the train came, but it would be enough, a promise. Afterward, Mathilde and I would leave the station together, arm in arm. We would send him letters in the same envelope, and his letters to us would arrive in a single packet, too.

Just as I stepped forward to go to Marcel, Mathilde put her hand on his wrist. Like any mother. As if every evening she kissed him good night, brushed his hair out of his eyes, rubbed his feet. She stroked his skin, a gesture so familiar, so effortless, that I could hardly breathe.

Their lives were with each other, and when he did fall in love, it would be with a girl as beautiful as Mathilde. My eyes stung, and I pulled my coat closed against the cold air, a coat that fit me as poorly as Marcel's fit him. I would have left the station, run out past the edge of the village and up into the high mountains, where the snow was still waist deep—but I couldn't tear my eyes from them.

Marcel looked down at Mathilde and she reached up to touch his shoulder. *Please, cheri,* she mouthed. *Don't go.*

Marcel shrugged her off so brusquely that she stumbled onto the tracks. I gasped, as mortified as if I'd pushed her myself, and when her face reddened, my own skin burned. She stepped back up onto the platform, smiling a little, as if she'd stumbled out of clumsiness. I wanted to run to her and apologize—for Marcel, for myself, for everyone who had ever been unkind to her—and for a second, I considered how I'd abandoned my own mother. She was back at our chalet, unwelcome even now, when the village was sending off its boys. When I was small, I had practiced my stitches with her every evening, trying to copy not just the fine motions of my mother's hands, but the shallow rhythm of her breathing. Now I barely noticed her.

Maybe Marcel did love me, I thought. Who could say? A boy who shoved his mother was not a boy who would reveal the tenderness of his heart, but when he came home from the war, when he tore my well-stitched clothing from my body, I would tame him and teach him to be kind. I'd do what his own mother couldn't.

The train pulled into the station—the same small, red train we took to school, already full of soldiers—and I noticed that the fog had burned off the valley. The boys would be able to look out and see the chasms below: the rocky cliffs and the stunted trees, the white, churning river at the bottom.

• • •

For the first few days after the boys left, the village was quiet. The mothers and fathers went solemnly about their business, and the very old grew vague, wandering the streets as if they had nowhere to go. But the young girls, dreaming of soldiers—we all walked a little taller, as if the world belonged to us.

On the fourth or fifth evening, as my mother and I sat in front of the fire, I spoke to her: "Maman," I said, though we rarely called each other by name, since we were mostly alone and didn't waste words.

She didn't look up from her sewing. Her hair in the firelight was beautiful, still brown and glossy as horse chestnuts, though she was past fifty, and if she'd not pulled it back so tightly, if she'd smiled more easily, she might have been pretty.

"Maman," I repeated. "I'd like to go to church."

Her sewing needle dove in and out, in and out, her thimble glinting. When she was done, she tied a knot, snipped the thread, and put the garment down; then she rose and went into her room. I thought she'd gone to bed. When she disapproved of me, she let me know by her deepening silence. After a few minutes, though, she came back, carrying the veil I'd worn to mass the year before my parents' divorce. She held it up, inspecting it with her small fingers, and then she pulled a white spool from her basket, mended its frayed edge, and handed it to me. It was so contrary to the way she'd acted my whole life—to what I thought of as her pride and stubbornness—that I realize now I didn't know her at all.

But I wasn't thinking about her then. I was only thinking of myself.

Mathilde was already in church when I arrived. I slipped into the pew behind her and, during the whole hour of kneeling and standing and sitting and kneeling, during all those cries of *Domine, non sum dignus*, I copied her motions, imagining that we were the same person, with the same fine hair and slender arms. I slammed my fist against my heart in time with her. If anyone stared at me, surprised by my return to the fold, I didn't notice.

After mass, I fell into step beside Mathilde and crossed the square with her. I waited in line with her at the boulangerie and, as soon as we'd made our purchases and were alone, I asked if she'd heard from Marcel. She gave a small, pained smile and shook her head. It didn't occur to me that she was afraid for his life. I thought she was dismayed because he was such a terrible son, and I wanted to console her, to let her know that, through me, she would always have him. It's just a mercy that I lacked the words.

Every Sunday of that sad, quick war, she smiled

at me, asked after my mother, and when she saw something that amused her—little Georgette Mathias trying to skip, a small dog yapping at a big one—she touched my wrist the way she'd touched Marcel's. *Look, Marie-Claire,* she said, chuckling. I tried to laugh the way she did, quietly, from the bottom of my throat.

In May, a sudden, windy snow-shower made it seem for a moment as if winter had returned; Mathilde and I paused outside the boulangerie and she raised her voice over the wind: "It's like being inside the mind of a madman. This whirling snow, without a point of rest."

Her complaint was so literary that I hoped she'd been like me—first in class, friendless, even homely—and as I wrapped my scarf around my head, I wondered where she was from, what sunny place that made a few hours of bad weather so alarming. It seemed indiscreet to ask, and anyway, the next Sunday was clear and warm. Just before we left the square and went our separate ways, she stopped by the fountain and nodded toward Mont Blanc. "I love it here," she said. "This cold, fresh air. And soon—June? July? When do all the wildflowers come out? It's the most beautiful thing I've ever seen."

"*You're* what's beautiful!" I burst out, and she laughed, touching my arm.

"Oh, Marie-Claire. You have no idea. All you have to do is stand up straighter." I turned bright red, and she continued: "And when you feel bashful, smile."

I looked away, still blushing, but the following Sunday, she sat down on the edge of the fountain and motioned for me to sit beside her. "You mustn't worry about your looks," she said. "A girl only needs a few tricks. Shall I teach you?" She went on without waiting for an answer: "At night, before you go to bed, rub salad oil onto your skin and scalp to make them soft. And here . . ." She took a lock of my hair and twisted it into a tight rope. "See how the damaged ends stand out? Twist your hair this way when you're at home and singe the flyaway ends with a match. Then brush your hair a hundred times. It will fall across your back like silk." She laughed then, and squeezed my hand, and I laughed, too, as if we'd shared a great joke.

I can't remember how I learned that Marcel had died. All at once, it seemed, the village knew, as if a flash had lit up the darkness and we had seen for an instant the whole geography of grief that lay around us—not only the boys who would die on the battlefield, but the ones our own police would later kill.

I stood in the corner of my bedroom, thinking, *Marcel is dead. He was alive and now he's not,* as if I were trying to solve an equation. I kept going over and over the same basic facts, getting nowhere. I was shocked, of course, and I cried, but more than anything, I was baffled. *He was alive, and now he's not.*

I should have rushed over to Mathilde's chalet, taken her something to eat, sat with her while she grieved; I should have done what any ordinary friend would do, but I didn't. The longer I didn't, the more impossible it seemed. It embarrassed me to think of her being inconsolable.

No one else went to her, either. Suddenly, I thought of myself as just another villager, and what did we really know about her? I told myself that if the Queen Anne's lace were blooming, I'd bring her some, but the Queen Anne's lace was still a month away. By the end of the week, Mathilde had left us.

No one knew where she'd gone, though the Widow Charles's son said he'd seen her on the road to Vaudagne. She had her suitcase, but he didn't ask where she was headed or for how long. When we went to the chalet she'd been renting from la mère Lagrange—I tagged along behind Nicole Lagrange and a few other women— we saw that she had closed the shutters and put everything away in chests so that the mice wouldn't eat them. The blankets and sheets and pillows and soap, a box of sugar and coffee and a few jars of jam (which we would come back to, of course, before the war was over) were all packed away and the mattresses tilted on their sides. She had weeded her garden, but even the tidy rows of turnips and radishes and carrots and potatoes, the heads of lettuce she'd left behind, did not suggest occupancy.

I thought of her, righting herself after Marcel shrugged her off, and I knew that wherever she went, she would tidy up the evidence of every injury that was ever done to her. She would hold no one accountable. I felt as if I would be sick, but Nicole glared at me: I had no reason to look so gloomy, she said. Mathilde had only been passing through.

Jean-Luc Coiffier died a few days later, and then Claude Mason and one of the Manets from Vaudagne. We lost the war in six weeks. We were in the free zone, but collaborators or *boches*, what difference did it make? They were two faces of the same evil, and though we didn't starve the way they did in the cities, we had lost our appetite.

And yet the leaves filled out on the trees and the forest rustled all summer long with its deep shade, its shifting light; the meadows filled with blueberries, and at dusk, while the valley exhaled the warm scent of hay and lupine, the snow on the mountains turned pink.

By '42, rumors of resistance were loud enough that even my mother heard them. The newspapers warned of Alpine terrorism and, though we'd always used the news for toilet paper, there was a special pleasure in it now. France would be redeemed by Maquisards. I didn't know who might be involved in sabotage, just as I didn't know who, besides our own government, was serving the enemy, but I suspected that my neighbor, Pierre Mason, was helping the Maquisards. I don't know why I thought so, except that he had always been a popular, outgoing boy, and now he walked with his hands in his pockets, his shoulders hunched, and spoke to no one.

Either way, I was proud of the rumors, but it wasn't until I was older and discovered that the British and the Americans thought we were all cowards that I became so fierce in my pride. At the time, what I mostly felt was an electrified awareness of the world—"fear" isn't the right word—and a dull ache of longing for my friendship with Mathilde.

Still, the way I'd wanted Marcel, the way I'd tagged after Mathilde, came to seem like the stuff of childhood. They were such simple infatuations—to see the pair of them walk by my window, with their heads nearly touching, had excited me in a plain, straightforward way. When three policemen burned to death in an abandoned chalet outside our village, what I felt was a darker thrill.

Of course, I *was* a coward. The kind our allies thought we all were. I kept my head down, followed orders, spoke politely to the police. I didn't want to let on that I'd only attended church on Mathilde's behalf, so I kept going. I wanted to tell my mother the truth, that it was a sham, but an admission like that would only have hurt her. She had loved mass, had trembled when she took communion.

She'd given her life to me and in my desperation to be like Mathilde, I'd forgotten her. I tried to make it up to her around the house, fixing her a tisane in the evening before she thought to ask, correcting her stitches without telling her, awakening before her to feed the fire so the house would be warm when she awoke, and she was grateful, but it was the gratitude you would show a stranger. I was part of the church now, and the church had cast her out.

In the spring of '43, around the same time that Pierre Mason and two other boys were taken in for questioning about the chalet fire, my mother began sewing a communion dress for Georgette Mathias. When it came time to do the smocking, she pricked herself—a thing she'd never done before—and then she put down her sewing, went to bed, and never got up again. Within a month, she had died.

I barely remember the days that followed.

I heard that our boys were still in custody, that three people had been hanged in Annecy, that the Désailloux sisters had given names, but none of it made sense to me. I knew only that my mother was dead. Old-timers, those of my classmates who are still alive, say that I went running into the road, crying; that when Nicole Lagrange wondered aloud if my mother had made her peace with God, I told her to go to the devil; that I refused all offers of food. I'm sure it's true, but I can't remember. What I do remember is my scalp stinging because I couldn't stop pulling my hair. To this day, if my comb snags, tears spring to my eyes and I remember my mother, her small, delicate hands brushing my hair when I was little, showing me how to do French braids for church, in the days when we still went together.

I left Les Houches as Mathilde had. I had never been farther than Chamonix and I went all the way to Paris. I have no idea what I was thinking. Paris was crawling with *boches* and the Allies were bombing the trains. No one traveled who didn't have to. Later, I told people I went to Paris to prepare for *l'aggrégation* so I could be a schoolteacher. That's what I ended up doing, but I can't remember what drove me there in the first place. For a while after my mother died, the world lost all its vividness for me. It's true that I've never understood the beauty of a city, but the buildings were draped with swastikas and there were German signs on every corner. You'd think that would have startled me, but after the first wave of revulsion, I barely noticed. The war had been going on for so long, and the buildings crowded in on me, the clatter of footsteps hurt my ears, and I hurried through the streets, trying to hear, see, as little as possible.

I took a small room in a pension near the Luxembourg, run by a toothless, wart-covered woman named Madame Charpentier who claimed she could not understand my accent. There was a flush toilet at the end of the hall, a luxury I'd never known, but I was so much colder in the city than I'd been at home in front of the fire. I made friends with one girl, Geneviève, whose room was next to mine—she was blond and delicate, a little like Mathilde, if Mathilde had been shy and awkward—but I ignored the other girls and they ignored me.

Mathilde herself is my only clear memory of Paris. I'd kept an eye out for her, hoping she might have moved to Paris after Marcel's death. I wanted to run to her and tell her that my mother had died. I thought that would make us equals! I imagined us rekindling our friendship, but I no longer wanted her to teach me to be beautiful. Now I imagined us both pale and plain, dressed in old clothes. If Mathilde and I could walk past a group of German soldiers, arm in arm, wearing our poor Alpine boots, I thought my mother would be vindicated. Everything in me was confused, the way it is in dreams, scraps of one part of life adhering nonsensically to another, as if my mother's willful poverty had been an act of patriotic resistance.

Mathilde wasn't in any of the places I looked for her—she wasn't resting in the Luxembourg or beside the river, where I often went to escape the press of the city. She wasn't hurrying down a side street, or waiting in a long line for some poor cut of meat. She was, predictably perhaps, in a dance hall, which I, just as predictably, wandered into by accident, looking for a toilet.

I could have waited until I got back to my pension or squatted in the shadow of a building. It was almost curfew and hardly worth getting in trouble for a toilet. But I went in, squinting into the darkness, the smell of alcohol. A few glittering, ropy-looking women were holding their dance partners against their breasts. If they let go, it seemed, the men would simply fall. There were no *boches*, just the slow, sad couples, the sticky floor, the smoke, and, at the front, on a dais, Mathilde, singing in her deep, lovely voice. I opened my mouth to call out to her, but I couldn't make a sound.

She held a microphone with one hand and stroked her breasts with the other, not the way a singer runs her hands along the side of her body, offering herself to her audience—none of the customers were looking at Mathilde, anyway—but as if she were soaping herself, lathering her body through the gauzy red fabric of her dress.

She was more beautiful than ever, with her hair cut into a bob, and her lips painted red. She looked ten years younger than she had in our village, dressed in those high-necked dresses with the little white collars, and her hair in a chignon. The other people in the bar may have been dissolute, but she was radiant, singing her song about the consolations of a kiss: *Le chagrin est vite appaisi, et se console d'un baiser.*

I wasn't shocked by her plunging neckline, the long slit up the side of her dress, or by the odd way she was touching herself—it cost me nothing, after all, to give up my fantasy of her innocence—I was shocked that she was still so beautiful, so much in life. I thought a mother who had lost her son should be a kind of phantom, biding her time until her own death. Mathilde swayed to her voice and a smile played around her lips, as if she knew that when she was done a man would come and claim her. I imagined that her smile would open as warmly as it once had when she saw me, and for a moment, thinking of those distant Sundays, I wanted to run up onto the dais and pull her out onto the street, take her to my pension and beg her forgiveness. I should have been with her when she received her telegram.

Le chagrin est vite appaisi, she repeated, her hand on her heart: *Sorrow is quickly soothed.* I slipped back out into the evening, as sickened as I'd been after we lost the war. How could she sing those words as if she meant them, as if she'd written the lyrics herself? She was no kind of mother at all.

But I wanted to talk to her, to tell her everything that had happened since she'd left. Maybe, I thought, if I told her how sorry I was that Marcel had died, she'd remember her grief and be a mother again. I stood on the pavement, equivocating in the mild, spring air, and it wasn't until I heard the sound of German at the end of the street that I remembered the time and jumped on my bicycle.

There's always a reason—a thousand reasons, if you want them, and afterward, a thousand regrets.

By the time the armistice was signed, I'd come down with tuberculosis and had been sent back to the mountains, to a sanatorium. That was where I met Pierre Mason again, when I had nearly recovered and he'd just been released from prison. He hadn't helped plan the fire, but they had found a Communist tract in his room.

He was bone thin, his head shaved and his

lungs racked. The men were allowed to wander the grounds as they pleased—the female patients could only go out as a group, with a nun to chaperone—and he used to sit on a bench and watch us take the air. One day, he lifted his hand. "Marie-Claire," he said. "Marie-Claire Sauvier!" I almost started coughing again, I was so startled that anyone had noticed me. They released me a few days later, but I stayed in a hotel nearby and visited him every day until he was well enough to go home, and then we went straight to the town hall for a marriage license.

Seven months later, when I gave birth to our first child, I thought I understood Mathilde at last: It wasn't radiance I'd seen in her at the dance hall, it was the sheen of someone who had been scrubbed raw. Mathilde had gone back to the person she was before Marcel, as if Marcel had never been. If he never was, she hadn't lost anything: in the gloom, she was a girl again, the world around her whole and smooth and featureless.

Now, I don't know. We never know how other people suffer, what sacrifices they make, what accommodations.

Perhaps my mother, far from being heartbroken when the villagers turned away from us, felt the dross of her life falling away, imagined herself becoming lighter and lighter until, at some longed-for point in the future, she would be as light and invisible as God. Maybe Mathilde just liked singing, liked touching her own breasts.

I only know that motherhood, like war, is all failed plans and improvising. Every generation builds its own Maginot Line and hopes for the best; the worst, until it comes, is unimaginable.

SOMEONE ELSE

I wrote to Docteur Naquet when Marcel was killed. He'd sent me money every month, his notes brief and formal, as were my replies. *Chère Mademoiselle. Cher Docteur.* I looked for a hint in his letters, some indication that he still thought fondly of me, and though I never found any, I was glad he called me Mademoiselle and did not pretend—as we all had—that I was a widow.

I'd been happy working for the Naquets. Every night, a hot bath; every morning, a bowl of hot chocolate. At home, there had been the orchard and eight siblings to tend to. A cold bath once a week if I was lucky, and no time for breakfast. My hands were rough, my clothes stiff with sweat and dirt, my face sunburned—but even so, my father said, I was prettier than my mother, who was unwell and mostly lay in bed. He said it angrily, as if my looks required him to do things he didn't want to do: reach under my skirt and down my blouse, pull me onto his lap, hide his face in my neck.

At the Naquets', I dusted, polished, helped Madame in the kitchen. Quiet work in a quiet house. The Naquets never argued or shouted; as far as I could tell, they never disagreed at all. I often eavesdropped: they sometimes discussed politics, but mostly they laughed, communicating in a kind of shorthand that was impossible to make sense of. In public, Madame Naquet was so reserved she seemed cold, but around her husband, her laughter went on and on; she had trouble catching her breath. She reminded me of Cleopatra—so dark and elegant—but he could have been a baker, round and simple with his round, popping eyes. She gave me books to read and she gave me days off for no reason at all except that the house was clean enough, she said, and I should enjoy the day. She believed everyone should have the chance to *develop*. Why, she asked me, as if I'd contradicted her, should a housekeeper *not* read, listen to music, visit museums?

When I had been with the Naquets for four months, she was called away to care for her father. The house seemed suddenly empty. The doctor retreated to his piano room in the evenings and I sat up in my room and read. After the first week, Madame Naquet wrote that her father's health was worse than she'd realized and she didn't know when she'd be back, so the doctor invited me to join him for dinner. We sat at opposite ends of the long table and I worried that I might be holding my fork wrong, but he didn't seem to notice. He praised every dish I set out—the fish with oyster sauce, the soufflés, the sole meunière, the soups, all things Madame had taught me to cook—and asked about my day. What could I say? The silver had needed polishing, the fishmonger had closed early? To fill the void he told me about his patients and when, after a few nights, I began asking questions, he always said, "A very good question," before answering me.

Within a month, I had taken on most of Madame's responsibilities: I greeted patients at the front door, organized the doctor's schedule, kept track of the medical supplies. When he was called out at night, I tried to wait up for him so I could make him a tisane if he came back before dawn, a coffee if it was time to get to work, but he often found me half-dozing on the divan in the front hall. I would jump up, embarrassed, but he just smiled and told me to rest. Once, when I didn't hear him come in, he carried me upstairs to my bed.

He began to tease me, but the way he did it was like a compliment, as if he was teasing some part of me that didn't know my own worth. I can't remember any of the things he said, only the feeling of my own happiness, up in my cheekbones.

Summer came, the long days and the warm wind, everything green and ripening. He found me fast asleep in the front hall again. "You can sleep with me if you like." He said it lightly, as if he was offering his coat, but later, when he touched me, his eyes welled up with tears. "You are so beautiful and perfect." He kissed my eyes, my mouth, my neck, my whole body.

We lived like man and wife until September—he brought me my breakfast in bed, and at night, he hummed to me until I fell asleep—and then his father-in-law died, and he left for three days to attend the funeral. I went back to my little room above the kitchen. My narrow bed with the white lace coverlet and the white lace curtains, the child-sized bookcase Madame Naquet had filled with books for me.

The day they returned, Madame saw me first. I was in the backyard, beating the rugs, and I wasn't well. I knew what the problem was—I wasn't stupid—but I hadn't faced up to it. Just as Madame opened the back door and called out to me, I leaned over and vomited in the grass. She stopped, and when I looked back up at her, standing in the doorway in her traveling suit, her face drained of all expression. She stared at me for a few minutes and then she turned and went inside.

I wiped my mouth on my sleeve and followed her. They were in the parlor, but the door to the front hall was open; I could hear them as well as if I stood between them. She hissed: "What's the matter with you? Raphaël! For God's sake, what is it you—"

"Claudine," he said.

"What? What, Raphaël?"

He didn't answer.

"I liked her, Raphaël. I liked her a great deal."

"Claudine."

I waited, holding my breath, but they seemed to have nothing else to say. What did I hope? That I could replace Madame Naquet forever?

"I'm sorry, Claudine," he said, finally. "I'm very sorry. It was stupid of me . . ." And then he said he would take care of things.

"I liked her," she said again, and I ran upstairs, not caring if they heard me.

He found me in my room. "Mathilde," he said, and he sat next to me on the bed and tried to hold my hands, but I pulled them away and looked past him toward the door. "I can make arrangements for you," he said, softly.

I studied the brass doorknob, the way the light from the window pooled on the carpet in front of the door. I thought if I stayed still, if I didn't speak, I could prevent whatever was going to happen next.

But I wouldn't give up the baby. I didn't want someone else holding my child. Feeding him, singing to him, teaching him his numbers.

For days, the Naquets murmured behind closed doors. I couldn't make out what they were saying, but in the end, Madame Naquet bought me a mourning dress and a train ticket. When I arrived in Lyon, where a friend of the doctor's met me at the station, he greeted me with all the consideration due to a young widow. I could tell the doctor's friend wasn't fooled—no one was fooled—but I didn't care. If the doctor wouldn't have me, what did it matter what anyone else thought? I knew how to look after a baby, I would manage.

Marcel was an easy baby, a copy of my youngest brother, so long and skinny and pink, with a tuft of red-blond hair on his crown. He made swimming motions in his sleep, like sea grass, his dreams full of vague smiles; when he began to talk, I laughed and clapped, and he laughed with me. But when he grew into a rawboned boy and went to school, he discovered that he didn't know how to fight like the other boys, and saw that I was useless to him.

My father had been right: my looks gave off a kind of poison. Men were too attentive, women suspicious, and in the school yard, Marcel bore the brunt of it all. We moved several times; each time, I thought I could convince people of my purity. I wanted them to think well of Marcel, to believe his mother was good, his father tragically dead. I made sure I never missed mass, I spoke little, but everywhere I went, people looked at me and saw disaster.

When the war came, I was scared, but I thought it would be quick. I thought we'd cripple the *boches* forever. It was quick, I was right about that. The *boches* killed our boys and in return we gave them everything they wanted. We were told to make ourselves stronger, more disciplined, more like *them*. Posters showed up everywhere upholding the family, that paragon of virtue: Happy father, happy mother, happy son and daughter. *Germany's victory is France's victory!* We'll throw out all the Jews and build a new and flawless state.

The Jews? Madame Naquet, offering me books, the doctor, snoring lightly on his back?

I don't know if Docteur Naquet wrote back after Marcel died. I'd moved to Paris and hadn't sent him a forwarding address. I didn't want anything after Marcel died. Not food or friends or comfort. I stayed in an empty shed in the Bois de Boulogne for a while and the only difference between day and night was that by day I sat up and by night I lay down. One afternoon, I watched a spider crawl down my thigh and drop by a thread from my knee before I thought to brush her off. I made so little noise that not even the *boches* noticed me. But in the end, I wanted to eat.

I work in a dance hall now and at night I let the owner do what he wants with me. He's mostly a dead weight, crushing my ribs. Sometimes I wish there were three of him, pushing down on my heart.

I'd like to tell the doctor about Marcel, not the

way I told him in letters—*Marcel is fine, thank you for the check*—but the real story: how rarely he smiled, and how, when he did, his upper lip caught on one tooth so that he kept smiling longer than he meant to. The way he would pull his knees up to his chin when he read, lost in a book. Detective stories, mostly. I want the doctor to laugh, ask me a dozen questions. *No,* I'd say, *he wasn't interested in medicine, but he drew beautifully. He looked like my people, my brother. He slept with me until he was four.*

I saw the doctor last week. I'd gone down to the river to smell the water, and there he was, walking toward me along the bank. His old, bright, sturdy self. I was so startled to see him here, in Paris, that for a moment I didn't notice he wasn't wearing a star. I thought he didn't recognize me. *Twenty years,* I thought, bitterly. *He can't see the girl in me anymore.* But then I understood: he was pretending to be someone else, a gentile. My whole body contracted, a fist in my stomach, but I managed to walk past him without making eye contact, without any recognition at all.

THE JEW AND THE GERMAN

Let's pretend you're the Jew and I'm the German. There has to be one of each: my great-uncle and the SS officer who arrested him. I've written this story dozens of ways, hundreds, always trying to imagine myself as my great-uncle. In photographs, he's on the verge of laughter, a moon-faced man with bright blue eyes. The kindest of men, everyone agreed.

After I've written the story, I picture my aunts setting fire to it. My aunt Françoise and my mother's aunt, Chouchotte. *You understand nothing,* they say. *Nothing! You weren't there, Polly, you can't imagine—and your Nazi! A cartoon! He insults us all. As if we would have been afraid of such a man.*

The war had been over for fifteen years when I was born, but, still, the sound of German unsettles me—in the metro, in a café. Tall, blond Germans my own age, laughing. I imagine them turning around, midlaugh, and shooting me, though I know it's wrong to suppose they're all bad. To imagine that I am wholly good. We are all everything.

I'll be the German this time, and you'll have to be the Jew.

• • •

Imagine, then, that it's spring, 1944. Chestnut trees are blooming all over Paris, and the flower beds in the Luxembourg have been laid in neat, geometric patterns. For the first time in years, you're not thinking about a leg of lamb, sweetbreads, a tongue and watercress salad. You're not preoccupied with the tiniest particulars of long-ago meals—the feel of a bread crumb pressed into your fingertip, the sheen on a pat of butter. Nor are you watching every shadow for the officer who will step out and order you to drop your pants. You aren't dreading the embarrassment you'd feel, with your underwear around your ankles, handing over papers that claim you're a gentile.

You're in the Luxembourg Gardens, with your easel and paints in front of you, but you can't remember setting it up. Apparently, your idea was to paint the fountain where, after the long winter, children are once again racing their boats. Their excitement fills the air, and you wish they'd shut up. You've always wanted a houseful of children, but now you want silence. The fountain isn't an original subject, but you're not an original painter. It's just a hobby. You're a gynecologist—one of the best in Caen—though you haven't practiced for three years; since you moved to Paris and became Vincent Leclerc, gentile, you haven't even owned a stethoscope.

Earlier today, Madame Compte, the concierge, hauled herself upstairs to see you: blue apron, red face, red hands. The war has cost her ten kilos, but she still shuffles like a fat person, and, because she's in menopause, she sweats profusely. She laughs that she's the only Parisian who doesn't mind the lack of coal, and you smile vaguely, as if you have no idea why she overheats.

This morning, however, she wasn't laughing. "Monsieur Leclerc," she said, and before she went on, you knew: Raphaël, your older brother, has been arrested. Madame Compte is the one who must have realized you were Jews, who must have informed on him. Maybe. Or maybe not. It's impossible to know. But if not Madame Compte, who? Hardly anyone else knows you and Raphaël are even brothers. Madame Compte will have informed on you, too, then. How else to explain the delicious scent of pâté and cognac on her breath?

But then, what? A wave of regret, and she came to warn you? And here you are now, in the Luxembourg, painting. It seems there's helium in your lungs, and where your stomach was, nothing, as if you'd been neatly eviscerated. And then your body rushes back into itself, a sensation of pins and needles, the blood in your veins so heavy that the effort of holding yourself upright makes you tremble. But still, you aren't thinking clearly. You've forgotten so much in the last few hours that it seems your life happened to someone else, an acquaintance you barely recall. You have no idea how you got to the Luxembourg.

Oh, Raphaël, who taught me everything I know. Who taught me nothing. Who, until he became his own gentile (Jean Carreau, landscaper), was a pediatrician in Caen. Eyes even bluer than yours, filled with more laughter. He was beloved by every mother who brought him a sick child. He loved those mothers in return and gave some of their children little bastard siblings. A half dozen boys and girls scattered around the Calvados whose Jewish blood's a secret.

On the north side of Paris, there's an empty house with a well-stocked attic. You can go there if you hurry. Tins and tins of food. More food than you've seen in years, to last however many years remain. Peas, asparagus, tomatoes, herring, pâté. Sweetened condensed milk. It was your idea. Chocolate and cigarettes. Food from before the war. No one else had your prescience. As soon as Poland fell, you remembered the rickets of your childhood and wrote to your niece in Paris: *Hoard. Store as much food as you can where no one else will find it. There's a place on rue Marcadet. You and your siblings will still be able to eat if the war drags on.*

She did what you said—the nieces and nephews hang on your every word; you're the young, fun uncle—but your sister, Suzanne, the children's

118

mother, sent her sons and daughters to America. And then Suzanne and your parents were arrested in the street, and you changed your name— Kaminsky, the forger, gave you and Raphaël new papers before you'd even asked—and you moved to Paris with one change of clothes and a set of paints. Raphaël found an apartment on rue Stanislas, you found one around the corner on rue Vavin.

You'd never intended that food for yourself, but who could you feed, once you were so newly, lightly, a gentile? So the attic with its stores became yours and Raphaël's, though neither of you went there, or spoke of the food, hidden away for the worst of emergencies; you barely spoke at all as gentiles, barely set foot in each other's apartments.

Clearly, your memory isn't completely shot. You can reconstruct the events of your life, even the events of this morning, if you put your mind to it, but so much is breaking apart; who can say which pieces are important? Madame Compte at the door, the news about Raphaël, the sight of your suitcase, already packed for just this moment—and then the circular staircase down to the lobby, the weight of the easel under your arm, right onto rue Vavin, left onto rue Guynemer. The bright spring air, the gates of the Luxembourg. Details as tedious to list now as the muscles of the foot, and as seemingly irrelevant: you're a gynecologist, after all.

Once, you dynamited a munitions train. You know this to be true, as you know that you're thirty-two, widowed, and responsible for various crimes against the state, including the distribution of pamphlets, as punishable an offense as the dynamite and the composition of your own blood. "Once" sounds like the beginning of time, but it was just two years ago, when you were still a Jew, before you went into hiding out in the open. After dynamiting the train, you crawled away under a blackberry thicket. There was a late frost, and you could probably see your breath, but that's too fine a detail to picture now; you can't imagine the weight of the dynamite in your hands, or the chill of the iron rails.

What you do remember, as vividly as if her scent were still on your hands, is Mademoiselle Maurois. Her thin, reedy voice, as if she'd never fully come into the world. You were barely out of medical school, but you had examined hundreds of women before her, and never with any desire; you hadn't guessed that desire could stun you this way, in the middle of an examining room with a speculum in your hand. *Docteur*, she said, in that small, empty voice. *My cramps. They're so painful that every month I vomit for a week.* You laid the speculum down and put your hands in your pockets, where you found a piece of candy, which you unwrapped and put in your mouth. Buying time. It's the candy you remember most clearly, butterscotch. Some nights, weak with hunger in your gentile apartment, you've thought of going to rue Marcadet and plundering all those supplies—you've eaten almost nothing but turnips and horse marrow for a month, and the rickets have come back—but you've always been able to resist temptation. You dip your brush, mark the canvas, dip again, mark, dip. Raphaël will be dead soon, you hope. You hope it will go quickly for him.

A giant marigold? That might be it, that smear of red on the canvas. And next to it, it seems, a tiny rubber tree. This isn't the way you paint. It's hard enough to paint what's right in front of you, to be faithful to the minute, incredible, shifting details of ordinary life: the flickering, silver underside of a leaf, the bones of a woman's wrist. Who could ever record such things the way they are? The blur of children playing. If you had the six children you've always wanted, you'd bore them to tears making them sit for portraits. Best not to picture a wife, but children—they're always a possibility. Six children by six different women or six by one: three boys followed by three girls. A house ringing with laughter, toys everywhere, music, squabbles. Maybe more than six. You might need to keep procreating until your oldest has children of his own, so there's always a tiny one underfoot, or sitting in a corner somewhere, a plump little Buddha, earnestly turning the pages of an upside-down book. Even so, you'd like the children at the fountain to be quiet. You yourself are very quiet, standing at your easel as if you'd been ordered to. As though, if you stood long enough, you might dissolve into the bright, windy day.

Years later, people will speculate about why you didn't run. He was too sad, they'll say. He was in shock. He'd used up all the adrenaline of a lifetime, and nothing further could alarm him.

Three and a half years of evading capture: even asleep, dreaming your fitful dreams of food, you were afraid. You'd see something on the ground—a glistening lamb shank, or a bowl of ice cream—and you'd bend down for it, but it was always a trick: everything revealed itself to be a yellow star, a kippah, a tallit. And how was that possible? A bowl of vanilla ice cream! Who could mistake that for a piece of cloth? You wept, trying to explain yourself, insisting the game was rigged, you ought to be given another chance. You sobbed, howling finally, and that was the stupidest move of all: if you would stop, they might forget about you, and you could slip away. You awoke on your back with your eyes dry, your arms frozen at your sides. There were variations in the opening scenes, but the end was always the same: the shouting, the pointless self-defense.

You slept two hours at a stretch, three at the most; the rest of the time, you were in the back room of your apartment, working on pamphlets, and little by little your heart stopped racing, because the typesetter was an old Linotype Model 8, half broken, and it required all your attention.

Until the day you transformed yourself into an ordinary, anti-Semitic little bourgeois, and then there was nothing to do and you were always afraid. Why lock yourself now in the half-light of the attic, and begin the infinite process of doling out smaller and smaller portions of tinned food to yourself so that it will last forever? Like the turtle in the arithmetic problem who, going always half the distance he went before, never reaches the wall.

Prisoner's Name: Raphaël Naquet. Alias(es): Jean Carreau. Race: Jew. Criminal Activities: Terrorism. List of crimes:
Somewhere in the city an SS officer is filling out the paperwork on Raphaël; it shouldn't take long, and when he's finished, he'll come for you. Who is this man, so hell-bent on sending you both to your deaths? Let's assume he isn't a monstrous aberration. Let's assume, given the endless repetition of atrocities throughout history, that he's an ordinary man. I have to give him qualities of my own, if I'm to *be* him, so let's say he has a headache.

He's already taken three powders, and he can still feel it, like a knife lodged in his eye. The light's too bright. Everyone raved about Paris in the springtime, how beautiful the light is; and Greta said, *Oh, the girls in Paris, you'll have a good time,* wanting me to reassure her. I have to imagine his wife, too: Greta. What he thinks of her.

No girl in Paris could compare to you, Greta, with your fat belly and your mustache. Spiess Walden says Paris is like a beautiful woman he's grown to despise. All he wants, he insists, is to go back to his little house in the country, be greeted by his dog like Odysseus, and spend a week in bed with his wife. What I want is never to have come here at all. I was happy in Berlin, working in the property division, and what is the ERR going to do now that so many of us have been conscripted? Someone needs to keep track of the inventory, and if we're all over here, tracking Jews, who will keep the books?

That was a nice job: a private office, the lamp with its green shade, the heavy door. I rarely had to speak to anyone. I only had to make sure that all the records were correct, that the value of the repossessed paintings and antiques and silverware and bank accounts was properly noted, that there were no misplaced commas, no careless errors. No one kept the books more beautifully than I. The Sturmbannführer praised my work, he said when the war was over he might hire me to run the mines with him. He's growing old, needs a younger man with a clear mind. But the Americans and the Soviets are closing in; they want us to be soldiers now, and this is a messy job. The job of a dogcatcher.

I'd take a fourth powder if it would help—hell, I'd swallow a cupful. But to go out that way, I'd like to be in a private room, not this cavernous office with the others barging in all the time. It doesn't seem like too much to ask. If I could just close the door, lower the blinds, I'd press a gun to my own eye.

I wouldn't want a French girl anyway, Greta. Even with a boot to the back of the neck, they let you know what they think of you. That little *tsk, tsk* of disdain if you don't hold your fork just right. I'd have bedded my own mother if I wanted that kind of scrutiny.

In Berlin, I kept regular hours, slept a decent night's sleep. Sometimes, at the end of the day, the Sturmbannführer offered me a brandy. I don't like brandy, but that isn't the point. It was an honor.

An ice pick seems to be sticking straight through my left eye to the back of my skull, and the light is bouncing off the walls like shards of glass. But I'm not crying. Note that my right eye is perfectly dry. When a man weeps, he weeps with both eyes. Still, I had to start over:

Prisoner's Name: Raphaël. I had to throw out two tearstained pages. I don't want a French whore as my reward, I want a dark room. I want to lie at the bottom of a cool, dark lake.

When Walden arrests someone, he ransacks drawers, riffles through papers, tips over a couple of armoires, and he's done. He never cleans himself afterward. I'm slower, but more thorough, and I touch almost nothing. There's no one here to appreciate my efforts, and still I do my best. I imagine the Sturmbannführer with his white gloves, his small, slow smile.

If I press my fist to my eye, I can think. I'd like to scoop it out of its socket.

This is the only thing that's wholly yours, these paints, shimmering in the sunlight: carmine, bone black, cadmium yellow. The thick, soft texture of the oil, and the brush, so light in your fingers.

You understand that for all intents and purposes, you're dead. You died when they arrested your parents and Suzanne and you had to become someone else, a little man who paints, who sits in cafés now and then, pretending to read the official news, though mostly you've kept to your apartment, painting the view from the window. It was better than hiding in an attic. If you couldn't work against the Germans, you could at least see the sky, the trees, the children racing home from school. You could go down

126

the street to the Luxembourg now and then. But your old comrades—your fellow *terrorists!*—don't know where you are, and you can't risk a radio. Only Raphaël knows you anymore. Knew. And the SS, of course. They know. If you run to rue Marcadet, they'll hardly give up the chase, and when they find you, they'll pause just long enough to gorge themselves on your food.

Which means you're yourself again, you might as well pin a star to your chest, but still, for all intents and purposes, dead. What remains between now and the moment you give up the ghost entirely are formalities—terrible formalities, it's true, but formalities nevertheless.

You pause, considering the marigold and the two red, fan-shaped petals you've completed. Is that what marigolds look like? There are none in front of you at the Luxembourg, and it's hard to remember. A yellow throat, or yellow on the petals' edges? Not a big, round, pom-pom marigold, you don't like those; you like to count the individual petals.

Yellow at the throat *and* on the edges—those were the marigolds your mother grew. One of the children bursts out laughing, as if she'd been following your train of thought and is delighted by its conclusion: *Yes,* her laughter says, *yellow at the throat and on the edges! Excellent! You've got it now!* Her laughter's quickly spent, but you still hear its bright echo, suspended among the boasts and reprimands of the boys and girls who are instructing each other in the proper technique for sailing a toy boat.

You gaze over at the children. It's already impossible to tell which of the girls laughed. The one with the long black braids? The little redhead? There's nothing funny about this business anymore. The boats are getting tangled up, someone's done something wrong—and yet, you still hear a girl's laughter, and you can't imagine having been irritated by the children. What could be lovelier than these stern little adults with their sailing missions? If you could— if you weren't dead—you'd steal the children away to rue Marcadet and give them chocolate, asparagus, pâté, whatever they want. Inside their mended socks and wood-soled shoes, you know, are feet still raw with chilblains.

The thought of pâté momentarily blurs your vision. A wave of hunger comes over you, as sickening as nausea. But that's just life, clinging to you in its cobwebby way. Still, all that food going to waste breaks your heart, which, mysteriously, will not stop beating, and so it's best to look away from the children, to focus on your marigold.

You brush a bit of yellow on the tip of one of the petals, and suddenly it comes to you: to be dead is to be weightless, a miracle! You wish it for everyone, even the Germans, why not, with their impossibly heavy boots. And yet, though the world is horrifying—so much rot and grief from the very beginning—how beautiful it is: light drifts down into the Luxembourg, onto the sandy paths, the lawns, the statues, the sparkling water.

And nothing further is required of you. You can stand here forever, dead, tending your marigold.

As if it's not enough to have an eyeful of broken glass, through which I still have to work, still fill out endless documents for a single arrest, I can't even sit here without needing to vomit. Another man might have given up, but I am not that man.

In Berlin, I had a migraine once a year at most, and I could go home, sleep it off, be back at work the next day. I didn't get any sleep last night, and I've still got the brother to find. Walden's already gone to the brother's apartment, and he wasn't there, so *I've* got to go and wait for him. Walden thinks nothing of making other people finish his work, and everyone tolerates it—admires it, even—because he's charming, with his sad, gray eyes and his smooth laugh. But I'll never get to the brother if I keep starting over with the paperwork, and I've got to get to him. Müller botched an arrest in the Marais and was gone within a week, sent to the front. It's not the fighting I'd mind so much if I were Müller—though the thought of the noise and filth makes my teeth ache—it's the humiliation.

If I could go back to Berlin, I'd close the shutters and lie in my own bed. Afterward, I might go to the Altes and sit for a while. I'd like to see the Berlin Goddess again, with her straight back, her pomegranate. Herr Grindberg kept me after class to tell me I should apply to the art institute in Düsseldorf. He loved my watercolors, he said, stammering, beads of spittle forming on his lips. In the corridor outside the classroom, Hans Lutz mimicked him for the other pupils. They laughed until they wept. How, Herr Grindberg asked, could I prefer numbers? I was thinking too much about my own father, he suggested, believing he was psychoanalyzing me when it was hardly a mystery of the psyche that I didn't want to end up like Father, with his execrable wire dogs that sold for less than the cost of the materials. Herr Grindberg said I was a true artist: *my* family wouldn't starve. *But I prefer numbers,* I said, clenching my fists. *I prefer the predictable, the real.* I hated being seen with him, standing beside his desk, forced to listen to his drivel. It wasn't Father I was afraid of becoming, it was Herr Grindberg, with his tongue flashing between his teeth, whatever dreams of glory he'd had worn away by the tedium of teaching boys whose only gift was a talent for mockery.

Mother wanted me to be an artist, too! Carting her cash to the grocer's, only to find out she was still half a million marks short of the price for a kilo of potatoes. If she'd chosen a more sensible husband, things wouldn't have gone so badly for her. They were all fools: Mother and Father drunk half the time, and Herr Grindberg with his wet, stuttering sincerity.

It's not a very good marigold. Alive, you preferred bluebells, rock jasmine, lupine. Delicate, alpine flowers with shadowy throats. But if it's a marigold you're painting, you'd like to do it well.

And suddenly, they're here: two of them in boots and armbands. Your hand freezes, the pulse in your neck is like a grasshopper, but the SS walk by, ignoring you.

The air around you is empty, suffocating; and then you dip a brush in the yellow, and your heart slows. Once again, your body comes back into itself with a sensation of pins and needles, but this time your blood isn't so heavy. You can hold yourself upright without shaking. You try to remind yourself that you're dead, but it doesn't work anymore. The blood demands to keep swimming through your veins, over and over through the chambered heart, feeding every useless desire: for pâté, women, a pride of children.

A single petal. If you can't get the whole flower right, concentrate on a single petal.

At last the shadows lengthen, a breeze lifts the hairs on your arms, and the children are called away, herded back to dinner. Mothers with painted-on stockings, bony hips. You could stay here, wait for them to arrest you in the Luxembourg, but you don't. You pack everything away, carry the wet, unfinished canvas back along the garden path.

There's no sign of Madame Compte in the apartment building, no sign of anyone, though it will be curfew soon and everyone ought to be heading home. It's as if they've been warned: *Monsieur Leclerc will be arrested tonight, you won't want to see that*. Wrinkling their noses the way the old doctor did when he examined that poor girl from Calais. Warts as big as brussels sprouts hanging off her labia, but what business did he have being a doctor if he had to look away? You've never had any patience for squeamishness. Yes, it will be ugly, you think, a couple of SS men carting away that nice painter, Leclerc. *A Jew! We had no idea.*

But you know it's simply chance, one of those moments when the world falls still, as if it had forgotten what it was about. There's no reason the lobby is empty, it just is; in a moment, everything will shudder back into action: *Oh, curfew! Oh, dinner!* And they'll rush indoors.

The windows of your living room are violet, dusk filling the city like water. The SS have been here—your books have been knocked off the shelves, your bed is unmade—they've come and gone. They'll come again. *We're drowning in this half-light,* you think. *If only night would fall.*

Raphaël must be dead by now. They won't send him to the camps, because they need information. *Please don't think this way.* Consider instead the blood's endlessly repetitive journey, and all you're leaving behind. Your whole youth, never to be revisited. Lupine and bluebells. The child you were, inside a boy's small, swift body.

All of them gone—Raphaël, Suzanne, your parents—and you saved no one, made no dent in this war. What good is a single munitions train and a few lost pamphlets?

Raphaël took you down to the river once and showed you how to skip stones. You were six or seven, Raphaël would have been sixteen or seventeen. For hours you practiced, far away from the house where your parents were fighting, where Suzanne sat in her corner, praying. Raphaël bent down, showed you the motion of his wrist, his arm, over and over.

"You're the only one I like," you said, and Raphaël laughed, ruffling your hair. "Nonsense. You love Maman and Papa and they love you."

"I don't love Suzanne."

"Suzanne's a pill," he said. She would have been eighteen or nineteen. Raphaël laughed again, as if everything were a joke, and then he lifted you up, swung you onto his shoulders, and ran along the riverbank. When you got home, a chicken was roasting and your parents were sitting close together on the couch, drinking wine. Suzanne sat across from them, telling them a story that made them all laugh, even Raphaël.

Or maybe that was a different day, with the chicken roasting. The skin crisp and salty, the juices soaking the little potatoes.

There's a knock at the door and your bowels soften, but you don't lose control; you walk to the door and open it as you would to a friend. Of all the people in the old cell—you, Raphaël, Kaminsky, Monsieur Girard, Jeanine Bonnet— you're the one who was most outraged by your countrymen's silence. *André,* Raphaël said, *they're terrified and hungry and they don't like us. They might not all wish us dead, but we are not one of them.* And now you open the door and nearly gesture to your guests to make themselves at home. Why give them the satisfaction of your fear?

There are three of them: two Milice and a German. The two Frenchmen are ordinary, middlebrow, one young, one old, both of them dreaming of their next meal. The younger one's jowly; the older has a wide, innocent face and a dimpled nose. The SS looks like all the other SS. Since they're required to have certain physical features, they can't even be considered clichés. The SS officer walks past you as if you're not there, leaving you and the Milice in the front room while he checks the rest of the apartment. If the younger of the two policemen were not aiming his pistol at you, you could leave. Run down the stairs and out into the watery evening.

The apartment doesn't smell. Most Jews' apartments have been closed up for so long, everyone hiding inside like rats, that the smell is awful. A terrible sickroom odor of fear I have to scrub off with lye. But André Naquet, he's been living out in the open like a gentile. No smell at all, not even the ordinary smell of an ordinary life. The brother was living like a gentile, too, but he'd had a woman—I could smell her in his bedroom with its big, rumpled bed—some whore who thought nothing of a Jewish dick. I loathe this job. I might as well be a schoolteacher, disciplining pupils all day. What's a teacher, after all, but a man in a strange land, forced to round up his inferiors?

There's nothing to find here: no odor, bare walls, a bag of turnips in the kitchen. Dishes washed and put away, the counters clean. In the bedroom, a single bed that Walden has already torn apart, and the windows open to the evening. A few clothes pulled from the armoire. A toothbrush, a razor, a towel. It could be a hotel. There's not even a headache powder in the nightstand. Detective novels scattered around the living room and canvasses against the wall— views of the street below and one, still wet, of a marigold—but no papers, no mementoes, no actual art. If it weren't for the books, I'd think he had just come for the weekend.

Still, there's no reason to rush. The men will guard him as long as I need, and I could rest. The Milice are here to serve us; why shouldn't I sit down? He may be a Jew, but this is a gentile's apartment. I could close my eyes, pretend there's a brandy waiting for me on the coffee table. Better yet, a bottle of beer. My eye doesn't hurt as much now, a dull throbbing.

Nicole, you think, and that's the worst possible thought. On the best of days, you avoid thinking of her. Twenty-two years old, thrown from a horse. You'd been married a year. Tall and beautiful, with her mass of long, black ringlets, her wild laugh. A Sephardi, much to your father's dismay. Your mother laughed at him. *Really, Victor? What do you care? We don't even celebrate Passover. What's it to us, one kind of Jew or another?*

They're superstitious, he said.

Be quiet, she laughed. *Better superstitious than small-minded.*

But when Nicole died, it was your father who sat up with you, night after night, when you couldn't sleep, when you shivered in the hot August breeze.

Everything that had been held at bay floods

136

through you now: Your mother used to sing to you, lying next to you in your bed, the smell of perfume on her wrists. On the morning of your sixth birthday, you touched her breast, though you knew you were too old, knew she would slap you away, but she didn't; she let your hand rest on her heart. You don't know if she's dead. You don't know if any of your family are dead. Some are starved and some are burned alive. Some are thrown still living into the ground. The full truth won't be revealed for a long time, but you know enough. Sometimes it's the thought of Suzanne, whose piety drove you crazy, that's most unbearable: the thought of her alive beneath a pile of bodies. Please let them all be dead. Let the whole world be dead. Spare us this grief.

And then you forget them all. The two men are smoking, and you're overcome with desire for a cigarette.

But the memory lapse is brief: you remember your wedding night, Nicole's dark skin glowing. Other women were lustier, more experimental, but no one else glowed. No one else made you dream of children. You took precautions before you were married—but on your wedding night, nothing held you back. You spoke of children every day, and whenever she had a bit of indigestion—she loved her pastries, mille-feuilles most of all—your heart sped up. No one else died so simply: a broken neck, and she was gone, the wide world unruffled by her absence.

What could be taking the German so long? There's nothing to find. No names, no documents, you're not a fool. Just a few books and paints. What's he doing? Tearing up the floorboards? But the only sound comes from the Milice, crushing their butts on the carpet.

What a delicious sleep. I haven't slept this well since I left Berlin. It must be past midnight. I'll have to get up soon, take the Jew down to the station, fill out his paperwork, but there's no need to hurry, now that I have him. The Sturmbannführer admired my deliberation. *You don't rush,* he said. *You understand the value of patience, precision.*

That marigold! As sloppy as a student's. He's even worse than Father was, but then again, he was a doctor; he doesn't imagine himself an artist. Did no one tell him we'd gotten his brother? He must be mad. He knows he's been found out, and he pauses to paint a marigold. Maybe I'll sleep a little more.

The young policeman yawns and holds the gun so loosely you could knock it from his grip. They're playing cards, and when he needs two hands, he lays the gun on his thigh. The German could have died in your bedroom, and the Frenchmen would keep guarding you until the last tank rolled into the last city.

It must be almost dawn, but you're still standing in the middle of the room, like a display. Something for sale. Again, there's a burning in your ribs, a sensation of breathing in smoke. You hear Madame Compte, laboring her way up the stairs, clutching the railing. On her way to the sixth floor for a little gossip with Mademoiselle Delunche.

The Milice open their bags and take out sandwiches. You want to leap on them, grab the bread from their hands; they'd shoot you before you touched their food and it would be a better death than what they have in store for you, but you're frozen, and it isn't the way it was earlier, when you stood, painting. That was madness, perhaps; this is the paralysis of fear. The ordinary, irrational fear that keeps a man who will soon be tortured from leaping to his death for a bite of bread.

This could be my apartment and I, a blessedly single man, watching the sky begin to lighten. The throbbing behind my eye has stopped. After I'd slept off a migraine, I used to be grateful, but now I know the next one's not far off. I have only the smallest window of time. A sliver of relief as thin as glass.

I'm stalling: I need to arrest the Jew. That's my

role in this story, a role I chose. *Forgive them, Lord, they know not what they do.* How else to explain our infinite capacity for evil? But I do know. I can describe more or less exactly what will happen to him in the camps, what has happened to the others I've arrested.

As soon as I get up, go to work, a new headache will sharpen itself into the back of my eye. It never fails. And what am I to do with a Jew who, faced with death, paints a giant marigold?

Which is the mystery? That a person arrests Jews, all the while thinking about his migraine and wishing he were home, basking in the praise of his Sturmbannführer? Or that André Naquet spent the day painting when he could have run? Naquet might be the greater mystery, but I'm the Nazi, not the Jew. I'm supposed to take him downstairs now, out into the armored truck.

I could punish him for painting. Push him over the balcony, beat him with my belt, the only thing that's forbidden is to let him go. I could put my gun to his head and demand an explanation. "I like to paint," he'd say. It's always something like that, something that doesn't add up.

Sure enough, my head's hurting again. It scares me to death when it starts and I don't have any powders.

Once, after Mother and Father died of their rotten livers, I dreamed I was flying. In my dream, I was back in my room at the university, and the window was open, calling to me as if I should kill myself. I went, spread my arms, and jumped, but the air buoyed me and I thought, *Of course, this was always possible.* All I had to do was spread my arms. I didn't go very high—there were buildings I had to circle around—still, I was airborne and when I awoke, I knew: I couldn't fly in this life, but I'd be able to in the life to come.

I doubt it now. Whatever greatness might have been mine isn't going to come to me, in this or any other life. The Americans have reached the coast; we've been sent to catch the last Jews because we're losing, and the Sturmbannführer will have no job to offer me when it's over. So why not keep sitting here a while longer, pressing my thumb into my eye? Or get up and paint a marigold! Why not?

What if I did? What if I set his canvas on the easel, squeezed the tubes of paint onto his palette, and began? And if, after fixing his terrible marigold, I let him go? Why not take my clothes off and dance a jig in the street? You can't stop what you're doing and change course. I mean *you*. You, Jew. I did, in fact, like painting. When it was going well, I hardly noticed the brush, just the image taking form. I might have applied to Düsseldorf, if I hadn't been so disgusted by Herr Grindberg.

You won't say what you were thinking even with a gun to your head, will you? How could anyone make sense of such a thing? You blow up train tracks, get word to people about what we're doing, pretend to be a gentile, and then, when you've been found out, you act as if this weren't a war at all. As if you thought yourself a Rembrandt. You go *outside* to paint. Where, Jew? Where did you go for your marigold? I ought to paint it over, a black square, just to show him.

Your mouth is dry and your legs are trembling, your hands. You've been standing so long—days, weeks, it's impossible to tell—and the Milice are still playing cards. You won't be able to stand much longer, your legs will give out, and you'll collapse on the floor, curled up like a dog, you think, your heart racing.

Carmine, bone black, cadmium yellow. The marigold with its fire-tipped, fan-shaped petals, its golden throat. I hardly know how to hold the brush anymore, and yet, stroke by stroke, the colors deepen, then lighten, then deepen again. The Sturmbannführer's promises meant nothing, they were as hollow as Herr Grindberg's praise, and how delicate the petals are, like the edges of a breeze. My left eye's leaking again.

The German appears and the Frenchmen leap to attention, but the German tells them to leave you—*Go!* he barks, a ragged yelp, and he follows them without a glance in your direction.

Your breath is so rapid it's like not breathing at all, until you see your finished marigold—luminous and perfect with its golden edges—and you understand that the attic on rue Marcadet, the chocolates and cigarettes, are yours. You haven't died. You wait until you hear the German drive away, and then you run downstairs and out into the morning. But you mustn't run in public, so you walk north across the city as calmly as you can.

In the attic, marigolds will haunt your dreams: your mother's hands, smoothing the dirt around their stalks before she pulls them up and offers them to a pair of SS officers. There are always two of them, identical in their tall boots.

When, after many months, you hear church bells, you'll go down into the street and the light will burn your eyes. You still won't know who's dead. They all are. The entire family, except your nieces and nephews in America. There's only you, in the burning light of a freed city.

And here's the deepest mystery: not that you painted when you could have run, not that the German let you go, but that you'll come to love the world again. You'll see pictures of the camps, learn how each member of your family was killed, a knowledge that shuts off your windpipe every time it comes to you, and it comes to

143

you again and again without end—and yet, the shifting light, the bones of a woman's wrist, the Buddha posture that is every toddler's elegance, will once more seem beautiful to you. You'll set up a new practice, marry a birdlike pediatrician who seems always on the verge of laughter, and who can quiet a crying baby in seconds. You'll be a friend to all your nieces and nephews, even to Raphaël's secret children.

But you and your wife will have no children of your own. You won't discuss it, though others—people who don't realize "Naquet" is Jewish—will mention the importance of rebuilding the nation, the maternal fulfillment every woman requires, the optimism restored to us by our progeny. You'll shrug a little, or your wife will. You might exchange a glance, though you won't need a glance to know what the other is thinking. Such excellent children you could have had! Smart, funny, beautiful. And so many names to choose from: your parents, hers, her siblings, Raphaël, Suzanne. But the problem is not exactly—or not only—the long history of Jewish persecution. The problem is how easily the world rips open, how closely darkness hews to light.

At last you'll be too old, and no one will bother you about rebuilding the nation anymore. Most of the world will be too young to imagine that you ever really had a life. Still, they'll adore you,

144

with your bright blue eyes, your grin, such a kind doctor.

At seventy, you'll retire to Ile d'Yeu, and in the ocean you'll find that you're as flexible as a boy again. You'll give thanks for all of it: the smell of the Atlantic and the shimmering taste of oysters and your wife's hair, fading from gray to white until it's no more than dandelion fluff. She'll make you laugh until your eyes well up with tears, and then she'll bring you plates of food so lovely they make you gasp. Every morning, you'll sit in the sand with her, wearing a cloth cap, shucking oysters, cleaning mussels.

AFTER THE WAR

ASH

Françoise has always been the quiet one, so good and amenable that at first no one notices her silence. Oncle Henri tells the others—Tante Chouchotte, Geneviève, Simon—about the weeks of digging, how they slept in the basement of the church with the rest of the town, how difficult it was to arrange the burials. He explains that they had to bury Yvonne in a suitcase because, by the time they found any part of her, there were no more caskets or lumber. After the war, he says, he'd like to move the graves down to Brittany, where Maman's people were from. His voice is measured and slow. He has had plenty of time to think about this, during the three weeks they spent in the rubble and the two weeks on the road to Paris, where the whole family is staying now, in Simon and Michelle's apartment.

No one thinks to ask Françoise any questions, until, one day, they do. The war is over; Françoise has had tuberculosis, gone to a sanatorium, returned. Simon and Michelle are divorced.

Michelle accosts Françoise on the street one afternoon as she's leaving school; she wants to know everything that happened in Caen. "Simon was never the same afterward," she says, though Simon was nowhere near Caen when

149

the house was bombed. Her eyes are wide with bewilderment and outrage, but Françoise shakes her head and hurries home.

She thinks the question is an aberration. Michelle is more erratic than ever, but who can blame her? Françoise thinks what Simon has done—divorcing her outright—is unforgivable. But a few weeks later, when Geneviève and Françoise are washing the dishes, Geneviève turns to her. "Do you want to tell me how it was?" she asks. "You can tell me anything." Her voice is lilting and gentle, the way their mother's was, but there's a hunger in it, too, and Françoise gazes silently down into the soapy water. For weeks afterward, Françoise can feel Geneviève watching her and then Geneviève meets an American, and is gone. She sets sail for America as easily as if they had never been sisters at all.

To console herself, Françoise considers that no one will ask her anything now. She marries a professor of history with a beautiful speaking voice. The things he talks about barely interest her, but she likes the sound of him, and she lets him go on, nodding and murmuring as she chops vegetables for their supper, heats the stew, sets and clears the table, washes the dishes. She dusts their apartment every day, sweeps and mops the floor, cleans the windows, and when he follows her from room to room, telling her about his lectures, the prizes he is being considered for, the people he has met, she wonders if there isn't a better way to remove the scuff marks from the floor.

"For the love of God," he says, finally. "Will you just sit? The floor is clean enough!" He's sorry, he continues, he didn't mean to yell, but he wants a wife, not a servant. An equal. He asks her about her past, explaining that they should have no secrets.

"There's not much to tell," she shrugs. "I'm not very interesting."

He sighs and, eventually, turns to other, younger women, who seem to have nothing to hide. Because he's a man of principle, he doesn't conceal his affairs and, when he's not with someone else, he still sleeps with his wife. What can she do? He's a man, she thinks, with a man's needs. She tries to do the deep cleaning when he's away, but since she doesn't always know when he'll come home, he often finds her on her knees, scrubbing.

For years, there is nothing. A stillness in her heart, as if nothing happened. As if she herself had not happened. She has children—a twin boy and girl, and then another boy, another girl—and she knits, she volunteers for charities—but all of it, the click of knitting needles, the meetings, the sight of her children asleep in their beds, seems like a shadow play. She knits more, collects more bags of clothes for the poor, organizes her children's holidays, oversees their schoolwork, but she cannot feel herself anywhere. It doesn't worry her because she can't remember anything else. She's a good person, she hopes. She has helped many people and her children are well behaved.

Every Sunday, she takes the children to have lunch with Oncle Henri, who beams at the sight of them and praises her for raising them so well. Then he sends the children out to play in the Luxembourg or, if it's raining, to explore the Louvre. She sits with him in the parlor, knitting while he reads the paper. This is her favorite part of the week, these hours of easy, companionable silence. He's happy in her company, he says, so she's happy.

The spring after Oncle Henri dies—her children are grown by now and out of the house—she's walking home with the groceries on a sunny day when the sky suddenly takes on a greenish cast. The air turns gray, cold, and the shadows on the pavement appear angular, like geometry problems. It doesn't last long—it's only a partial eclipse—but her vision blurs and her legs are so weak that she stops in a café and takes a seat in the corner, as far from the door as possible. When the waiter comes, she orders a hot chocolate, though she has not drunk hot chocolate since she was a little girl, and she needs to get home with the groceries.

For days afterward, she is sore and irritable. Her skin is too sensitive and her eyes hurt, as if she is coming down with the flu. When she begins to cough, she hopes it's not a recurrence of tuberculosis. The cough doesn't worsen, but, still, there is something inside her, dark and poisonous, that makes it hard to breathe. She wonders if she has cancer, if she might be dying, and is surprised that the thought doesn't trouble her. She wouldn't mind dying, she thinks, but the moment she thinks it, she knows that's not it, and is filled with despair.

Memory floats through her like ash.

She remembers, now, being thirsty. She remembers piles of rocks and a stone floor, the plaid of her mother's apron. Glass shattering in another room.

The images coalesce: utter blackness, and then twilight. She thought Oncle Henri was a ghost, and then she blinked the dust from her eyes and saw that she, too, was covered from head to toe with a fine, white powder. People were running in the street, all of them coated white, all racing toward the church.

Dust sifted from their eyes, their ears, their mouths, onto the floor of the church basement, and the nuns' habits dragged through the dust, turning white and soft, as if their hems were trimmed with fur. There was no food that day, and only small amounts of water.

All afternoon and into the night, they sat in the basement, listening to the explosions up above, the blast-force crashing of the windows in the sanctuary. In the morning, Oncle Henri told her to stay put, but she crept behind him, back toward the house. He didn't see her until it was too late—what could he do? It would be as dangerous to return as to keep going. Bombs fell on the horizon, the sky lit with flames.

When they had pulled the first beam from the rubble, he scrambled down through the shards of glass, the stones, and wept. Maman lay beneath a broken window frame, hardly bruised at all, her arms thrown over her head, little half-moons of sweat staining her apron.

There are other memories, too, now, older ones: her siblings playing in the garden, Maman and Oncle Henri drinking coffee in the shade of the apple tree. She remembers the honeysuckle growing up the side of the house, and Yvonne's laughter, the way it tumbled out of her, sending her running to the privy. *I'm going to pee, I'm going to pee, I'm going to pee!*

She could not get the dust out of her lungs; it clogged her windpipe for days.

When she saw what was left of Yvonne, she

screamed. "Sh-sh," Oncle Henri murmured. "Sh-sh. Try to be brave. You're my only child now." He lifted the arm from the ashes and cradled it as if it were an infant, indifferent to the smell of it, rotting red and purple in his arms. "You're all I have left," he said, his eyes bloodshot. "Do you understand, Françoise?"

"We have Geneviève," she said, trying to control her voice. "Geneviève and Simon." But Oncle Henri shook his head, as if he did not believe in Geneviève or Simon.

At night, Oncle Henri held her as close as her mother always had, and she clung to the sturdiness of his body, the tightness of his arms.

She has no memory of her real father, who died when she was a baby, though she remembers sunlight streaming in through the slats of the nursery shutters, Yvonne singing to her dolls, and Maman telling Yvonne to hush.

The darkness in her lungs, the flulike symptoms, come and go for months, but she does not succumb to them. She keeps the house clean, prepares her husband's meals, delivers food to the poor.

One day, when her husband is spending the weekend with a girlfriend, she hears her mother's voice as clearly as if Maman were holding her, a murmur next to her ear, and she sits down on the edge of the bed and weeps.

• • •

After they'd found Maman, after they'd carried away the broken window frame and picked the shards of glass from Maman's hair, Oncle Henri carried Maman out to the garden. He went back to the house to look for the others, but she stayed in the garden with Maman. Soot drifted onto Maman's face, her arms, her chest, and Françoise brushed it away with her own soot-blackened hand. She has never loved another body as much as she loved her mother's.

She's sad for a long time after she hears her mother's voice, but everyone thinks it's because of her husband's too-public infidelity. Her children tell her not to put up with it; Simon disparages the whole institution of marriage. Geneviève knows nothing of what's going on, she lives in North Carolina, married to her American; but Geneviève's old friend, Marie-Claire, invites Françoise to the Alps for a change of scene. Why not? she thinks. She likes Marie-Claire. They were in the same sanatorium for a while, their beds side by side.

She watches the evening light wash across Mont Blanc from Marie-Claire's balcony and drinks too much of the blueberry liqueur Marie-Claire offers her. She hears herself talking on and on about her husband's mistresses, as if she could possibly care about them! But she cannot shut up, she has turned into a chatterbox. She thinks of Oncle Henri, and realizes that he's the only person she wants to talk to, because he carried Maman to the garden, because he cradled Yvonne's arm without flinching. She remembers the way he called her, Françoise, his child, and she wonders suddenly if she was.

She begins to shake and Marie-Claire puts a blanket over her, asks if she wants to go inside, but, despite her drunkenness, the way the balcony rocks and the mountains vibrate in the distance, she holds her tongue, finally. It's all with her now as clearly as if the planes were still diving overhead: the smell of the fires, the blackened rubble, Maman's perfect, unbruised body. She can see the sooty tomato vines growing beside her mother, hear the terrified, starving chickens, the scrabbling rabbits. It was all a lie, she thinks, the house with the honeysuckle and the garden in back, the flock of chickens, and the fat little rabbits. Her older siblings busy with their lives—Louis and his girlfriends, Simon and his books, Geneviève playing the violin, and Yvonne always getting into trouble—while she stayed by her mother's side, the dutiful one, her mother's best girl. The bastard child.

She stumbles to her feet, certain she'll be sick, and Marie-Claire tries to follow her, but she pushes her away. In the bathroom, she kneels over the toilet, a fifty-year-old woman, heaving air.

But in the morning, she wakes from a dreamless sleep with nothing more than a headache and a dry mouth, retaining nothing of the previous evening except the vague sense that she was a fool. Then she remembers that she suspected her mother and Oncle Henri of having an affair before they were married and she laughs harshly: a cheating husband has made her imagine the worst of everyone. She hopes she said nothing about it to Marie-Claire. No, it was the girlfriends she went on about. What nonsense!

On the trip back to Paris, she's lulled by the train's rhythm, the rushing fields. But then she thinks of Oncle Henri again, ashamed that she doubted him and doubted her own mother. It's stupid to dwell on the past; it's too far behind and you can't see any of it clearly. What appears over your shoulder to be a turtle might have been a hat! Best to put it all out of your mind, once and for all. She'd allowed herself to wallow in the past, and what good had it done? It had given her a cough and made her skin hurt, that's all.

She reaches brusquely for her knitting basket, determined to get hold of herself, but she can't shake her regret, the sense that she has wronged the two people who raised her to be what she is: a decent, hardworking wife and mother. And Oncle Henri wasn't even obliged!

Well, then, when she gets to Lyon, she'll change trains. She'll go to Pornic, where the family plot is, and tidy the grave. Throw away the dead flowers, replace them with a pot of something that will last awhile. Ivy. She nods, happy to have made up her mind, and then she pulls out her knitting needles and casts off.

THE RANSOM RING

Tante Chouchotte said America was too far to see: what Polly was staring at so hard that she was going to ruin her eyes was not land. That strip of blue at the edge of the long gray ocean was only more water.

Tante Chouchotte didn't like Americans. Polly's mother had married one—a cellist, of all things!—and left the family forever. Polly's mother came back for the summers, but she spent the whole time in Paris, scattering her children around with friends and relatives in the countryside: the older ones, Evie and Louise and Pete Junior, to Marie-Claire's, in the Alps; Polly to the beach with the little cousins.

Polly was a pill—*une pilule*—gloomy and solemn and given to crying over nothing at all. Her siblings had gone to the countryside for the summer as soon as they could speak— Tante Chouchotte herself had taken care of them when they were babies—and their French was perfect, but Polly was five and this was her first summer with Chouchotte. Last summer she had still gone everywhere with her mother. Imagine! A four-year-old traipsing around to the kinds of cafés and bars Geneviève was known to frequent. Geneviève knew nothing of the work of disciplining children. She'd had a charmed life, Tante Chouchotte said. That was the trouble with her.

And Polly had nothing to be sad about: the beach was lovely. If Polly had lived through the war, she wouldn't keep asking to speak to her mother, as if you could just use the telephone whenever you felt like it, for no particular reason. The telephone was for grown-ups, it wasn't a toy. If Polly had *known* the war, she would hush.

Polly had drunk the war in with her mother's milk; she loved stories about the Germans. At home, in North Carolina, her mother had a box of shadowy, scallop-edged photographs. The pictures were taken in a garden, and the people in the photographs sat at a round table beneath an apple tree, their faces tilted toward the shade. Polly's mother would pull the photographs out one by one and hold them in her palm. *This is your tante Françoise, and this is your grandmother; this is your step-grandfather and this is your tante Yvonne. It is not real coffee they drink—we have no coffee, only chicory—and there is no sugar to make a canard.* The people in the photographs had been bombed a little later in the summer, buried beneath the rubble of the house, but you couldn't see the house in any of the photographs, and when Polly was older— seven, eight—she would wonder why the family hadn't stayed safely in the garden. But now, she questioned nothing except the horizon.

The box of photographs was kept in a trunk, and next to the box, nestled in bits of old flannel, was a thin, rusted helmet with a ragged hole in its side. *No one is knowing I have Louis's helmet,* Polly's mother said one day, sitting on the floor of her bedroom, her back against the trunk. She was holding Polly in the *V* of her legs. *You don't tell. Here,* she said. *You hold the helmet. Not the photographs, only the helmet. The helmet is strong.* She pulled Polly up onto her lap and laughed the way she did when she was sad. *Not enough strong, but even so, strong.* Louis had been her older brother. She put her hand on Polly's forehead and stroked Polly's hair; then she ran her fingernails lightly along the inside of Polly's arm until Polly shivered and laughed and buried her face in her mother's long, smooth neck.

She was not like other French mothers. She told Polly secrets, let her do whatever she wanted.

Polly stood at the edge of the ocean, her toes in the water. Yellow foam swirled up around her ankles and the cold sand pulled out from beneath her feet. Before her, small waves broke against the shore, turning white and frothy for a moment before collapsing; except for the glide and call of the seagulls, the sky was empty. Her mother would have let her stay there forever if Polly wanted, listening to the birds and staring out over the glare of the ocean at what was so clearly land, home. It was night in America—Polly believed that, though the horizon was clear and light—and she thought of the windows open and the sound of the whip-poor-wills.

Farther up the beach, beyond the seaweed and the driftwood, near the barnacle-covered rocks, where families lounged with umbrellas and towels and straw baskets, the other cousins were filling pails with sand, collecting shells, submitting willingly to an endless loop of scolding. There were six cousins altogether and, except for Polly, their names all went round and round: Jean, Jean-Marie, Marie-Jeanne, Jacques, and Jacqueline. All of them had dark, curly hair and deep suntans and they sang songs Polly didn't know. Even the twins, Jacques and Jacqueline, who were four, knew the songs, and only cried if they fell down. Their mother was Tante Françoise, but the others—the Jean Maries—were second cousins. They spent all their holidays, even Christmas and Easter, away from their mother. The Jean Maries adored Tante Chouchotte, and the lemon and orange taffy she kept in her pocket, which she doled out grudgingly, as if the children would not stop pestering her for it, though they never had.

Polly kept her gaze fixed on the horizon. If she

looked at the others, and they looked back at her, she might burst into tears, and Tante Chouchotte or Tante Françoise would be mad. She would not be able to see America, how it shimmered in the distance.

Bonjour, Polly! Êtes-vous Americaine? her friends would howl, later, when, as a teenager, she told them how much she'd hated her summers on the coast of Brittany—the sagging woolen bathing suits and the squat toilets, the casual swatting of thighs and bottoms, the snake-bite precision of a face slap—how she had missed America, with its broad, white, gleaming sidewalks where a child could play whatever she wanted till the sun went down. She'd loved America when she was little, in the 1960s, with everything so new and shiny, all the pretty shopping centers and swimming pools and televisions.

A lifetime later, her friends, stoned out of their minds in the weedy, abandoned parking lot of one of those early shopping centers, could not stop laughing: *Parlez-vous Français? Mais oui! Où est la Tour Eiffel?* they cried. *Ici!*

She rolled her eyes, but if a handsome boy was in the group, or a popular girl, she'd explain that she was a French citizen. She was known for her skill in lying to adults, so that a handsome or popular newcomer might think she was making it up—she'd sat in the back all through French

I and French II, never once raising her hand—
but her other friends, the ones who knew her,
vouched for her: *She knows all that conjugation
shit backward and forward.*

In fact, she was a dual citizen, which did not
suggest quite the same level of chic—of fashion
sense and sexual capability—that being purely
French would have, but it wasn't a lie, either: she
was French, and it pleased her to be two things
at once, to contain two worlds, which she could
move between freely, secretly; it was a kind
of currency, earned during all those long, sad
summers with Tante Chouchotte.

Now she stood perfectly still and quiet, but it
was not enough to stay still and quiet. She must
play with the other children. *Viens jouer avec les
autres*! Come! A pail was thrust into her hand
and a wave of pure grief rose in her chest—
she thought of the silky hair at the base of her
mother's neck, how her mother would let Polly
twirl it around her finger—but she kept her eyes
open, unblinking.

The grown-ups sighed when she mentioned
her mother, they made low, guttural sounds of
disapproval, or raised their voices, but they
did not slap her as quickly as they would have
slapped one of the others. Nine months a year
in the States, an American father, a careless
mother: Polly had no table manners, she couldn't

pronounce her *R*'s, she said *le maison* and *la chat.*

Qu'est-ce-que t'as enfin? What's wrong with you?

Polly was silent. There was no answer that could satisfy. She tried to think of one, but her throat was too full, the sky too bright and empty.

Pourquoi t'es toujours si triste? Why, Polly? Why are you always sad?

She thought of the war and imagined a chair beneath a bare bulb, the adults all leaning in over her: *Pourquoi? Mais pourquoi?*

Is that possible? At five? To imagine herself being interrogated that way? They were better than Mother Goose, all those old, romantic stories. Adventures of bombs and rubble and danger. The prisoner tied to his chair. *If you had known the war, you would hush! Oh, if you had known. If only you had known!* She *wanted* to know.

Why, Polly?

She knelt down where she was, and began scooping the hard, foamy sand into her pail.

Not here, Polly! Come join the others! What's wrong with you?

As if a person could ever answer that question. To answer incorrectly is as dangerous as not answering, unless you can come up with a diversion. Her mother had explained it all to her: how bravely people lied when the Nazis

167

were at the door, when they themselves faced torture. *Torture,* Polly. *The Germans put the gun to their face but they never tell what they know. If the Nazis ask where is somebody, they invent a story. They make a diversion.* Polly's mother spoke English, because Polly's father didn't like listening to French. But he didn't mind when she took the children to France for the summer. He couldn't practice with the kids making a racket all the time. His practice room was in a separate little house in the backyard, but still the children's noises made him want to buy a firearm. *Oh, Peter.* Polly's mother would laugh. *Do not say so.*

Tante Chouchotte grabbed Polly's wrist and Polly followed Tante Chouchotte's heavy, varicose-veined legs up the beach. She liked varicose veins, blue as the sky—her mother had them, too. Polly's mother was a butterfly, Polly's father said, laughing. She couldn't settle on anything, could she? The violin, tennis—what was it now? Papier-mâché birds? Polly's father laughed. *I can't keep track of you, Jenny.* Her mother blushed. Her blond hair was piled on top of her head and she wore a tiny gold cross on a gold chain. On her hand was a large diamond ring. But she did not like it when people cried, either. *When the Germans come, no one cry, nobody make a fuss. You will have a nice time at the beach with Chouchotte.*

Tante Chouchotte's fingers dug in Polly's arm, but if she could make a diversion, Tante Chouchotte would let go. If she could make a story to distract Tante Chouchotte from the question of why she was sad when there was nothing to be sad *about*. That was how it was done: they tied you to a chair and asked you questions; they might ask where your mother was—*Imagine, Polly, asking children to tale-tattle their parents!*—but if you were very clever, you could get rid of them. You could send the Nazis on a *wild chase goose*. Polly's mother loved American turns of phrase; whenever she used one, Polly's father laughed and pulled her onto his lap; he smelled her neck and hummed.

Monsieur Schwarz liked her mother's neck, too. He was her mother's friend in Paris. When they visited him, he offered Polly a bowl of dragées. They were baptism candies and Polly's mother thought it was funny that Monsieur Schwarz liked them. *Ces bonbons de baptême! Ça te fait plutôt prêtre, Rémy.* It makes you seem like a priest. A Catholic! When she laughed, she touched his cheek; then she turned to Polly: "Monsieur Schwarz and I, we have important business that is not for the children. The dragées, they are for you, but when you are big, there is always some important business. It is very boring, so you eat the candies and when I have finish we go to the Luxembourg."

In French, Monsieur Schwarz said her English was atrocious.

Les affaires m'ennuient déjà, Polly's mother murmured, but she was laughing, so Polly knew that she wasn't actually bored.

Polly did not like the dragées. She didn't like the hard shells or the almonds inside, but they were very beautiful—pink and blue and cream-colored ovals—and she lined them along the arms and back of the leather sofa in Monsieur Schwarz's living room, so that it looked as if it were studded with jewels. Then she explored Monsieur Schwarz's apartment. There was a balcony off the living room where she could stand and watch the cars and people in the street below; she stuck her feet through the railing and leaned out into the breeze, lifting her arms, and then she went in the kitchen, where Monsieur Schwarz had a fridge. It wasn't as big as the one at home, but it was a real refrigerator, with a freezer and boxes of frozen food, and Polly stood for a long time, gazing at the cold steam coming off all the neat, square packages. It was the only refrigerator she had ever seen in France, and it made her happy, as if Monsieur Schwarz owned a small piece of America. In the bathroom, even lovelier than the refrigerator, was a roll of soft, pink toilet paper and an actual toilet with a handle instead of a chain. She pressed her fingertips into the paper and sat up on the toilet, but she didn't have to pee, so she went back to the living room and admired the dragées on the sofa. She did not go in the room where her mother and Monsieur Schwarz were; it sounded as if they kept trying to lift something very heavy, and then, after a long time, her mother sighed, as if at last they'd set it down.

When her mother and Monsieur Schwarz opened the door and came back into the living room, they were both smiling; they said the candy arrangement was exquisite. Monsieur Schwarz claimed he would leave it the way it was forever, but Polly said that was impossible: as soon as he sat, he would ruin it. "I will never sit," Monsieur Schwarz said, in English. "I do not want to change anything." Then he touched the diamond on Polly's mother's hand, murmuring that the ring had grown loose—wasn't she eating?—he must take it and have it fixed; but her mother said she would take care of it herself, and then, suddenly, she looked like she was going to cry. Polly held her breath, but her mother didn't, she didn't cry, she just kissed Monsieur Schwarz's mouth. He stared right down at Polly without smiling, as if he were mad, but then he closed his eyes; he kissed Polly's mother's throat and put his hand on the back of her neck.

Afterward, Polly and her mother did not go straight to the Luxembourg. There was a café at the end of Monsieur Schwarz's street, and Polly's mother held her on her lap and ordered a grenadine with ice, which she pressed to her face. "Do you know what we do, Monsieur Schwarz and I? When you are big, there are hairs on your leg and you must take them off. Monsieur Schwarz, he puts a wax on my leg to take the hairs away. It is painful, but very necessary. It is a *soin de beauté*. A beauty care. Can you say this? *Un soin de beauté?*"

Even in France, Polly's mother spoke to her in English, so that they would understand each other perfectly.

No one—neither Tante Chouchotte nor Tante Françoise, nor anyone else—ever asked Polly where her mother was, but if they did, she wouldn't tell them about the *soin de beauté*, because you must invent something clever, so that the interrogators who have tied you to a chair, who want you to betray the ones you love, race off in the wrong direction. *If someone is at the South Pole, you tell he is at Alaska. The story has to be the same in one way—very cold—but the contrary. Then you are believed.* If Polly was clever enough, the interrogators would leave her alone for hours, days, maybe. She would be able to wiggle her way free—to loosen the ropes, slip

172

out, run away; she would hide in the woods until the war was over.

For years—long after Tante Chouchotte was dead, long after Polly was past the age of homesickness—that was her fantasy: how, if she'd been born earlier, she would have escaped the Nazis. She pictured her own brilliant survival on roots and berries and then the heartbreaking, stunning reunion when she wandered at last out of the forest. She slipped from tree to tree, making sure it was safe, and it was, *she* was— and, oh, then, the joyful, tearful reunion: *Polly, you're alive!* The weeping and offering of treats (a slice of cake, a bowl of chocolate). *How did you do it? How? Oh, Polly, our darling, our beloved, welcome back!*

That's enough sulking. *Ça suffit.* You have a *jolly pail,* now make something nice like the other children. Jean, who was seven, looked at Polly briefly before flipping over his pail of sand: he had made a perfect tower. He was the oldest and Polly liked him the best of all the cousins. Jean-Marie, who was six, was chubby and quiet and Polly neither liked nor disliked him, but she despised Marie-Jeanne. Marie-Jeanne was a month younger than Polly and she would only speak to Jean, as if they were the two grown-ups and no one else counted. Sometimes she carried Jacqueline around for a while and talked baby talk; then she'd put Jacqueline back down and talk to Jean in her regular voice. She whispered to him, took his hand and pulled him away from the others, laughing.

Polly knelt in the sand, scooping it into her bucket. It was hotter up here, away from the water, and her shoulders stung pleasantly. The Jean Maries were teaching a rhyming game to the twins, who squealed whenever they got it wrong. Sometimes, when they played a game, Marie-Jeanne said Polly should be on a team with the twins, as if she were a baby, too. Polly wished she could tell Marie-Jeanne that *she* was the baby; she wanted Marie-Jeanne to know that at home Polly could do anything she wanted, and her mother told her secrets, but she wasn't sure how to say all of that in French. If she said something wrong, she would just sound stupid.

Tante Chouchotte and Tante Françoise lay a little bit away from the children, on their beach chairs, gossiping. Tante Chouchotte was really her mother's aunt—she was old and fat and she wore a black dress, even at the beach—but Tante Françoise was Polly's mother's baby sister, though she didn't look it: she had dark hair and big, floppy breasts. She did not like children, she said. Babies were one thing, but children were impossible.

Tante Françoise was in the garden when the house was bombed. Polly's mother had been in Paris that day, but Tante Françoise saw everything: she stepped out of the toolshed onto the garden path, and the house exploded in front of her. Polly must never talk about that in front of Tante Françoise. Tante Françoise didn't like stories about the war.

Polly did not mind filling her pail over and over again: she could do it quietly, glancing every now and then at the horizon. She was not upset when her towers crumbled because she could keep making them, and the time would pass, the towers adding up like minutes. Then the morning would be over. In twenty mornings, she would see her mother.

But the grown-ups said the towers were silly, they ought to make a castle. What's the point of all these towers lining the beach? You can do better than that. Make something beautiful.

Une jolie pelle. Not a *jolly pail,* a pretty shovel. The day would never end.

You must come up with just the right answer for the interrogators, the one to throw them off the scent, because if you say the wrong thing they'll know you are lying and then the punishment is too awful to imagine. If, instead of saying Alaska when your mother is at the South Pole, you say Mississippi, for example, they might know that's wrong. If they already know she's somewhere cold, then you are in more danger than before.

Polly could spell Mississippi and she knew where all the states were on the map. She knew the states and the North Carolina tree and the North Carolina bird. She could count to one thousand. But in French the numbers confused her and she could not spell at all; she didn't know if any bird was more important than another.

So many tales of bombs and rubble and prisons and torture; in all of them, salvation depended on the right story.

The others set about making a castle, but Polly froze. Her mother did not believe in telling children how to play or what to make. *Interrupting somebody's belief-make—make belief?—it is a crime!* She was a musician, not like Polly's father, because she didn't practice when she didn't feel like it, but sometimes she played small chamber concerts—Polly always pictured a chamber pot—and when Polly and her mother wanted to be alone, her mother would tell everyone that she was preparing for an audition and not to be disturbed. She and Polly would curl up together on the big bed, preparing love auditions, her mother said, laughing.

If anyone telephones, Nettie, say to them I prepare a big performance.

What if it's someone you do *perform with, ma'am? Won't they know?*

I am permitted to play with more than one

orchestra, am I not? She laughed. *Say to them I make birds then. Or perhaps I cut my fingernails—or I am dead!* She laughed again. *Say I am dead.*

But still they spoke of love auditions, and Polly lay in her mother's arms while her mother dozed. Pete Junior and Evie and Louise teased Polly for napping with their mother, for always having to be the last one to kiss her good-bye, the last to say I love you. Polly's mother said not to worry about what the big children said, and Polly never did: she could watch the sun fall across her mother's body, lighting the hairs on her mother's arms. A dogwood rasped against the sliding glass door at the foot of her mother's bed, and it thrilled Polly that her family owned one of the state trees, and that sometimes a cardinal tapped on the glass.

Jean was calling out instructions about the castle, how to build it so it would last. Polly did exactly what he said, thinking they might be friends— you had to dig deep for the wet sand, and pack it hard—but he kept whispering with Marie-Jeanne, and suddenly, when Polly didn't expect it at all, tears were streaming down her face, slick and oily on her salt-dried skin. She made no sound, but Tante Françoise caught her anyway: What is it? What are you crying about? And Tante Chouchotte said that's enough now. Do you want me to slap you? Which was another impossible question to answer.

Polly thought frantically of auditions. If there was an audition she could say she needed to go to—anything she *had* to do so that they would leave her alone—but there was nothing. Even when she went to the bathroom, Tante Françoise or Tante Chouchotte accompanied her. She was too little to go into the ocean by herself, so if it was just pee, one of them would carry her in and hold her legs open in the water. Otherwise, they would take her by the wrist and walk with her up the beach to a little cabin with a hole in the floor and a few squares of wax paper. Tante Chouchotte stood in the doorway, staring out to sea, but Tante Françoise gazed down at her to make sure she was wiping properly.

Polly said nothing. She scooped sand from the moat but ended up putting it in the wrong place, and Jean-Marie pushed her out of the way. Tante Françoise yanked him up by his fat, sandy wrist. Couldn't he see that Polly was sad? Why did he have to be a bully? Jean-Marie's eyes turned red, as if he might cry, too, and Polly's throat burned; but when Tante Françoise walloped him, his eyes stayed perfectly dry, he did not even flinch.

Then it was time for snack. *Un petit goûter.* An interlude, their father called it, when they had *goûter* in North Carolina. No one was mad while they ate; Polly chewed the soft bread and sucked on the square of chocolate and no one scolded her. Tante Chouchotte and Tante Françoise discussed the afternoon's plans between bites.

There were many things to do, because the day was eternal: the cemetery, lunch, nap, the market, and still the sun would be high in the sky—but Polly loved the cemetery; they went straight from the beach, carrying their pails and shovels, and holding hands so no one would get hurt. In the cemetery, everyone was quiet and everything was laid out in rows like in America. Long straight paths and between them, the square marble slabs. Even in the older part of the cemetery, where the pocked and blackened slabs were different sizes and often tilted, the paths were straight, and everyone was quiet. There was a nice smell in the cemetery, something dusty and fresh, like seagulls.

The family stone was high and wide, like a big bed, with many names. Tante Françoise and Tante Chouchotte stopped talking. All the children had to do was look at the stone and not make any noise. It was an easy thing to do and even the twins knew enough to stand still.

Polly could read her own name, "Pauline," on the stone—that was her grandmother—and beneath "Pauline," "Yvonne," her mother's sister, who died when she was sixteen. Yvonne was Evie's name, too. Her mother had named all the girls after people who died in the war.

In the photographs in the box at home, in North Carolina, Grandmère Pauline and Tante Yvonne leaned into the shade, their faces speckled with light. You couldn't see Tante Françoise's face, because she was leaning against Grandmère Pauline, her head on Grandmère Pauline's shoulder, her face turned away.

When I am young, I am a serious musician—it is difficult to believe, but I am! That is why I survive the war. We are living in Normandy, but I go to Paris for an audition. The audition, it is schedule for the six of June—I am not saying a lie!—so I am not home on D-day. I am in Paris playing the Bach Chaconne. I am too fortunate! This is why I survive. My family, they are everyone bombarded except my little sister Françoise.

It was Polly's favorite story. Her mother told it over and over, holding Polly on her lap and reciting it whenever they had guests—other musicians, artists, her mother's papier-mâché teacher. It was the only story that never changed. Other stories had different endings, depending on who was listening, but this one was always the same, so that Polly knew every breath, every pause, by heart. The guests gave low whistles, or said *goddamn*. Afterward, there was always a long silence during which Polly's mother held her close and she could smell the Nina Ricci her mother put on for company. She could feel her mother's pulse in her throat, and below that, hard and steady against her ribs, her mother's heart.

Polly would rub her thumb over the polish on her mother's fingernails and play with her diamond ring. The stone was big and the band was platinum, but if you covered up the diamond, it looked as simple and plain as a metal washer. Polly pulled it off and tried it on her own fingers. Once, when no one was looking, she put it in her mouth. She kept very still, so that she would not swallow the ring, feeling the weight of the diamond on her tongue. Then she let it slip forward, and she curled her tongue through it. The band clicked against her teeth, and the taste of the metal made them ache. She was afraid it would slide off her tongue and back down her throat, but she could not let the ring go, holding it in her mouth as if it were a living thing.

It was very expensive, her mother said, but it wasn't an engagement ring. It was a ransom ring. She had bought it for herself after the war so that, if she was ever captured, she might exchange the ring for her freedom. *That doesn't make sense,* the older children said, every time. *What if the interrogators kill you?* Her mother shrugged, but Polly was certain the ring would work. *The beauty, it is a diversion. You offer your beauty, and you are free.*

She held out her hand and Polly slipped the damp ring back onto her finger.

Françoise, she dig under the rocks for the body: my mother, my grandmother, my sister Yvonne. She has not found Yvonne, only her arm.

If there was no company, the children could draw the story out: *Tell us again where Tante Françoise was standing, why she wasn't crushed. How did she know it was Yvonne's arm?*

Polly wanted to lie down on the tombstone, that wide, flat, sun-warmed rock; she liked seeing her own name and Evie's, and she felt as if the stone belonged to her, as if this were her home and Tante Françoise and Tante Chouchotte were merely guests.

She thought of Tante Yvonne's arm and pictured her sister's, tan and muscular because Evie played tennis, with the ring Evie had gotten from the gumball machine at the A&P. Evie had promised the ring to Polly if she could ever get another one to drop down. Polly imagined a hinged box, a velvet-lined case, like the one in which her mother kept her violin. In it, the arm lay whole and smooth and smelling of Johnson's baby oil.

But it was time to go. Tante Chouchotte blew her nose and Tante Françoise glared at the children as if she meant to spank each and every one of them.

• • •

After the cemetery, after lunch, Tante Chouchotte herded them upstairs for a nap, swatting them and lifting herself painfully from step to step because her legs were swollen; she closed the shutters in the long room with all the beds and told them to shut their eyes.

As soon as she was gone, the Jean-Maries began whispering. Polly lay on her back, staring up into the shadows, breathing in the damp, salty air. She wouldn't have minded lying quietly; she could have closed her eyes, pretended her mother was right beside her—but Jean and Jean-Marie and Marie-Jeanne and even the twins' high, whispery voices tightened around her ribs and throat, so that it was hard to breathe, and then there was a square of light in the room: Marie-Jeanne was calling down to the grown-ups, telling them that Polly was sad again.

When she awoke, she was alone. The shutters had all been thrown open and she could hear the others in the yard below, playing the rhyming game. They were laughing, their voices ringing out into the afternoon light, and she realized all at once that she understood the game, as if, while she slept, she had crossed over, become fully French. She lay with her hands on her chest, breathing fast—it was like being home, to understand so perfectly—and she did not want to be left out anymore; only she didn't want them to turn and look at her when she came down, she wanted it to be as if she had always been one of them.

She made her way down the long staircase, trembling with the strange, new sense of her own Frenchness. At the bottom of the staircase, the tiles were old and uneven and Polly was careful not to step on the cracks, but she hurried through the deep gloom of the kitchen, the soot-stained ceiling so low she'd be able to touch it in a few years, half-running as she wove between the stove and the *garde-manger* and the pail of scraps she could smell more than see. You weren't allowed to run inside, but she had missed so much already, and she threw open the back door into the brilliant afternoon sun: the flagstones burned her feet, and she squinted, opening her mouth to join in the game—and stopped.

They had disappeared, vanishing at the sound of her, it seemed, and though she'd only loved them for a few minutes, she cried out, alarmed—even though she knew better, knew it was only a trick of light, and she could hear their voices—and then they came into focus, appearing in the sunshine as swarms of dots until they solidified, became colorful, animate—

Mais enfin! Tante Chouchotte said, furiously. Why are you yelping? Did you step on something? A little rock? You should have put your shoes on. Go get them and you can play with the other children.

Tante Françoise stood up, the flat of her palm in the air. That's enough, *ça suffit*. You wear me out.

The others paused, waiting to see if Tante Françoise would spank her.

But then it came to Polly, the answer, the thing she could say that would throw them off her scent just long enough to allow her to escape into the woods: "My mother called me." *Ma mère appelle moi.* She could feel that there was something wrong with the way she'd said it, but they understood her.

"What?" Tante Françoise's hand was still in the air. "Qu'est-ce-que c'est que cette histoire?" *What kind of story is this?*

"She misses me." *Elle manque moi.*

"What do you mean?" Tante Chouchotte asked. "What do you mean, she called you?"

"She called me on the telephone." The sun warmed the top of her head.

"The telephone?" Tante Françoise's hand floated down, as if something about the telephone itself upset her, as if she wanted a phone call, too.

"She's very sad."

"The telephone rang," Tante Françoise said, "and you answered it?"

"I'm very worried about her." Polly knew exactly how to say that people were sad or worried in French. *Je suis très inquiète.*

"But why didn't you tell us the phone was ringing? Why didn't you say anything?" Tante Françoise was still standing, but her arms hung at her sides, and her voice was strangely high-pitched.

"I picked it up." *J'ai ramassé.*

"You answered the phone," Tante Chouchotte said sharply, as if Polly had done something dangerous, like turning on the stove, but still no one corrected the way Polly spoke. "Why didn't you tell us?"

"I knew it was her, I knew she'd be in a hurry."

Tante Chouchotte waved her hand as if she were shooing a fly. "*Qu'est-ce-que c'est que cette histoire?*" What kind of story is this?

"She told me she would call, so I knew." She wasn't cold, but her teeth had begun to chatter, and she dug her fingernails into her palms to stop them.

"The telephone rang," Tante Chouchotte said, "and you answered it."

"I knew. She told me she would call." *Elle dit à moi elle téléphone.*

Tante Françoise sat down heavily. "*Elle m'a dit qu'elle allait me téléphoner,*" she murmured, offering a correction at last. "What did she say?"

"She said she was very sad."

"What is this nonsense?" Tante Chouchotte kept shooing the air.

"She said she was sad because she misses me very much."

"Your mother called you on the telephone to tell you she was sad?" Tante Chouchotte shook her head as if there were a plague of flies.

"Yes."

"You answered the telephone?" Tante Françoise sighed.

"I knew it was her."

"Do you think—?" Tante Françoise turned toward Tante Chouchotte: "Would Geneviève telephone from Paris?"

Tante Chouchotte's head shook more and more slowly until, finally, it stopped altogether. "It's possible," she said after a while. "Who knows what she would do?"

The others had started rhyming again, but now they added in new twists, the way people do with rhyming games, and Polly had to strain to make sense of it. Tante Françoise and Tante Chouchotte weren't looking at Polly anymore, so she sat on the ground at their feet: when they talked about her mother, it was as if her mother was there.

C'est quand même intéressant, said Tante Chouchotte: it *was* interesting.

Crois-tu que Geneviève est triste? Peut-être ce Schwarz—? Tante Chouchotte and Tante Françoise leaned in close to each other, the way Polly and her mother did when they had love auditions. Was Geneviève really sad? Had

Schwarz—? Tante Françoise reached down to hand Polly a sugar cube dipped in coffee, a *canard*. What could Geneviève have to be sad about?

Years later, smoking with her friends beneath the broken awning of the old shopping center, Polly remembered that afternoon in the yard in Brittany as the occasion of her first lie, when she'd discovered how simple it was to fool everyone. She laughed out loud then, a wave of near-hysteria rising inside her. *I've been lying my whole fucking life—my mother tongue is deception!* But even stoned, she knew that wasn't right: her mother tongue was an accent. A confusion of vocabularies and place: *this is not where I should be, this world, this part of the country, this side of the garden.* What she had known from the beginning was the language of dislocation, its meanings bent and scattered, like light, into a kind of iridescence.

She sucked slowly on the sugar cube, feeling it dissolve in her mouth, and she was suddenly sleepy, though she had napped a long time; but the sun made her drowsy, the sun, and the rhyming voices she could no longer keep up with, and the faint hum of knowledge that her life had begun: she was learning to invent stories, as elaborate as her mother's, and as radiant as any jewel.

THE VISIT

Why bother? I could scour the sink, wash the windows, the walls, mop the floor, climb up on the table to scrub the ceiling, and the place would still seem derelict, as if a shut-in lived here. *Chouchotte Laurent, you know her? She went mad when she was young, had to be sent to the Salpêtrière. Afterward, she went back to teaching, but you should have seen her apartment. Cigarette ash and dead flies everywhere, books scattered all over the floor.*

I don't want André to see me living like this. André Naquet! They gave him the Médaille de la Résistance after the war. He'd been part of a group in Caen, blowing up train tracks, I had no idea. I wonder if I wrote to him then, or if I wrote when I learned his family had died. I hope I did. Who was it who told me about the Médaille de la Résistance, anyway? What living person knew we'd been acquainted? Not that they'd need to know, it was enough that we'd all come from Caen. Month after month of naming our dead, until we had named them all and could begin to name our heroes.

I haven't laid eyes on André since the twenties. It's 1965 now. Forty years. And suddenly I get it into my head to invite him to tea! *Tea,* as if we were British! There he was, in an old address book, so I wrote to him. It's been forty-*three* years. I'm seventy-seven, I was thirty-four when they let me out of the Salpêtrière, twenty-eight when André and I were lovers. He was nineteen, barely older than my students. I had no business with him, but I couldn't resist, telling myself that a young man needs an older woman, though André was born already knowing anything I might teach him. Night after night, I insisted I had classes to prepare, and he just laughed and pulled me into bed. He had an easel in his bedroom and he'd paint me in the mornings when I was too sleepy to object. Amateurish paintings that I loved for their sincerity, and the way he stood at the easel, tilting his round head from side to side. He wasn't handsome, but he was beautiful the way all the Naquets were, with their startling blue eyes and their olive skin. Every member of the family possessed a grace and confidence that no one, not even Pauline, with her rosaries and her tidy house, could resist. Baking all day for Raphaël and thinking no one would notice!

But which part was I remembering when I invited André? Our few months in his bed near the university, or the Salpêtrière, where he found me, six years later? We were lovers, and I threw him over to marry a man my age; and then, when I landed in the hospital, when he owed me nothing at all, André visited me. He was very kind and now I'm going to serve him tea.

I don't think I was remembering anything. It was an impulse. An old woman's foolishness. I cannot stop my hands from shaking. People say they feel this way—this anxiety—when they're in love, but when I was near André, I felt something different—a dissolving, a weightlessness.

I'll run down to the florist's. Get the place cleaned up and fill it with flowers. Lilies, roses, an armful of sunflowers. Potted geraniums for the windowsills. And I'll buy pastries from Dalloyau—of course! But I need to hurry. Wash the dishes, shake out the rug, sweep the floor. If I focus I can clean the whole place in an hour—it's not an actual apartment, just a long room with a kitchenette on one side and a sitting area on the other—but is there no more dish soap? Scrapings of hand soap, then.

No doubt he doesn't care about a clean room. He's sixty-seven, his parents and siblings killed long ago at Auschwitz. How a person goes on living is not the mystery. Terrible things happen to you, and they might put you in the Salpêtrière for a while, or they might not, but either way, you eat, you drink, you take a little air. Hold yourself apart, from yourself most of all, so that you don't bump into anything, the terrifying dreams and the bits of memory. The mystery is *why*.

He wrote back right away—*how nice to receive*

your note, I should be delighted to have tea— just like him, so polite. The thought came to me yesterday that I should tell him the truth about the Salpêtrière, why I was sent there. I've never told a soul, but suddenly I felt that André should know. He should be made to understand that the pity and kindness he showed me at the Salpêtrière was misguided. But to what end? To show him that the world is even darker than he imagined? What can that do except add to his suffering?

And then again, perhaps he won't care. Why should I and my crimes matter to him after what he has survived?

Look at me! An old, fat woman with not one dress that isn't stained. And I've nothing to scrub the sink with. It's good that I have old newspapers. They make a mess of the hands, but there is nothing better for cleaning windows. No streaks at all, I should have been a charwoman. There—what a difference, to be able to see the trees so clearly, the young people ambling along the sidewalks! Roofs of cars glinting in the sun. It's like getting a new pair of glasses. God willing, this chair will hold me and I can get the upper panes. If I can keep my balance.

My son, Bernard, climbed on everything. He never broke a bone, though, never even bloodied his nose. When my husband was shot at Château-Thierry three months after our wedding, when my infant daughter died of the flu—none of that could have been helped, but Bernard was another story. I fell asleep by the river. We'd gone there for a picnic the morning of his sixth birthday, just the two of us—we were all that was left, after his father and sister had died. My strong little Bernard, with his thin, blue lips, and the swampy weight of him in my arms.

It's nothing. The chair didn't break, and my ankle's fine. Not even a sprain, just a little throbbing. I can walk on it perfectly well. But this floor! It's caked with dirt. I should have thought of that before I washed the windows and let the sun pour in all over everything. I should have told André to meet me in a café!

I still don't know how he found me, who told him I was at the Salpêtrière. My gown was falling open in the back, a detail I remember not because it embarrassed me, but because it seemed the whole world might rush in from behind. There's no safety in an open-backed gown. André would have been in medical school by then; perhaps that's why they let him see me. Many times, he came and sat beside me on the stone floor, his hand on my knee. We never spoke. I couldn't— hysteria, that was my diagnosis. *The patient does not utter a sound.* The doctors tried to hypnotize me, inquisition by a swinging watch, as if a perfect recollection of my sins would ease my suffering. Between sessions, they ordered the lights dimmed and the food bland to ready me for the next trance, but they made no progress; I would have spoken to get rid of them, but I could not find my voice. Nothing but a dry trickle at the back of my throat. André just sat, his breath beside me steady and mild. He took my arm one day, lifted me to my feet, and led me out to walk the grounds; my feet swung awkwardly, uncertain where to land. It was a bright winter day, the paths sparkling, and the branches of the trees as smooth as metal. I'd been given my own coat to wear and a pair of my shoes. It had surprised me to see them, those pieces of my old life—the little buckles on the shoes, the coat's fur collar. I shrank from them, but André helped me with the sleeves, and then he knelt and slid each foot into its shoe. Afterward, he walked with me whenever the weather was fine, until I was pronounced well enough to leave the Salpêtrière. I'd learned to sound words again, though I never said what the doctors wanted me to say. I could not confess that I'd fallen asleep.

I was sent to my parents' home to finish recuperating. My mother hovered nervously and my father flinched at the sight of me and I didn't stay long. On one of our walks, André had given me the address of this studio, with its view of the Luxembourg all along one wall and its sleeping nook behind a curtain. No hallways, no doors opening to empty rooms. I never thanked him. I have lived here for forty-three years, letting the dust turn to grime and I did not even send him a note. I hope I wrote to him when I heard about his family, but I'm not sure I did even that much.

So much is lost: Who I spent time with between the wars, what I did on the weekends, besides grade papers. Even the second war is blurry. I remember how nervous I was, bringing potatoes to my colleague when she was hiding in a basement on rue Jean Bart, and I remember Michelle running down the street, calling out the names of the dead as if she'd triumphed over them. Little else. It's the war of '14 I recall; it's always a person's first war that stays with her. My hospital volunteer's apron over my pregnant belly, and the stunning smell of gangrene.

The windows are shining, the dishes done, the floor swept. This will have to do. Flowers, then, and éclairs from Dalloyau. My back hurts—these bones weren't meant to carry so much weight. It's a miracle I didn't break the chair. If I can find my purse—there—and now down the stairs. Madame Silva is sweeping the entryway, bent in half so that her torso's parallel with the floor. She still pushes her broom morning and night, keeping a low eye on the comings and goings.

"Madame Silva," I say, brightly. The more ordinary I seem, the less she pries into my life.

She stops, rests her shoulder against the broom handle and grunts hello without lifting her head. "You're going out?"

"I'm off to get a few things from Dalloyau. I have company coming." But as soon as I say it, I feel a wave of nausea. What can we talk about, André and I? What did we ever talk about, besides our desire for each other?

Madame Silva shrugs at the floor, resumes sweeping a little pile of dust, which scatters in the breeze when I open the front door. I want to apologize, but I hurry out instead.

In the Luxembourg, the pigeons strut their iridescent breasts, the trees shiver from green to silver and back again. I'd like to spend one more summer here before I die, but I promised Françoise I'd help with the children. And I do like the train ride to the coast, with the view of the sunset over the water and the damp, salty wind coming through the windows. If it weren't for the children, I wouldn't mind going to Pornic for the holidays, but the little ones wear me out with their frenzied jumping, the way they scream every time a wave comes. I've never much liked small children, except for Geneviève. So pale and quiet, with her enormous eyes, her thin arms around my neck. I love her still, but I hardly see her now. She rushes off, leaving her son and her daughters with anyone who will keep them; she barely seems to miss them. They're difficult children. The older ones can't go five minutes without hitting each other and Polly weeps at the sight of me.

The only children I loved completely were my own. Even with the soldiers' cries echoing into the maternity ward and my husband dead, I was so happy when I learned I'd given birth to twins. Two children make a family. Curled together in the crib, as they'd been in the womb, Thérèse sucked Bernard's thumb.

But here is Dalloyau, with its bright little door chime and the smell of chocolate. Shopgirls in their crisp white coats, like doctors. I ask for two miniature coffee éclairs, two chocolate ones, two raspberry tarts, two lemon tarts, and a box of caramels.

The florist's is impossible—such a profusion of colors and smells, and it's difficult not to stroke the petals, the waxy ones and the velvety ones, the silken ones that have barely unfurled. I settle on a dozen apricot roses and a small bouquet of lilies of the valley. In the thin mirror around the florist's door, I am a beggar woman with my gray hair, my long, dirty dress, but a beggar with flowers, with a beautifully wrapped package from Dalloyau.

The Luxembourg is full of students now, murmuring in pairs, their heads bent earnestly together, hands clasped behind their backs; little boys shouting by the fountain because their boats are going sideways, falling over; and at the merry-go-round the old man is scolding his customers. The light dapples onto the garden paths and floods the street outside the gates. I'm holding my packages carefully, the box of pastries in front of me, the flowers cradled gently in my left arm, so that nothing will get crushed, which is why I don't see André standing at my door.

How is it that we recognize each other? But we do. My hands are trembling again. I need to tell him something, but I can't think what.

"Chouchotte!" he exclaims, smiling the way he always did, a secret grin. He has his own pink-edged roses, of course. That's how it's done, the guest brings flowers. "Let me help you." He takes my apricot roses and the lilies of the valley, adds them to his bouquet, and kisses me on the cheeks.

"You're here," I say when he steps back.

"I just arrived." His hair is graying at the temples and there's a shiny bald circle at the top, but his eyes are unchanged—those round, laughing eyes. Geneviève's are the same shape and color, a blue so rich they seem to have been painted on, though hers never laugh. "This very minute," André adds. His aftershave smells of lavender.

"Come in," I say, my heart leaping. I don't know where to look, but the key always sticks, so that's something to concentrate on. "I wanted to have you over for tea," I add, stupidly. My gaze is still fixed on the lock, even though I've found the spot where the key catches. I detest it when people state the obvious. *I wanted to have you over for tea!* "There! I always have a bit of trouble, but I manage it eventually!" I laugh, determined, it seems, to play the daft old woman. "I always manage!"

Madame Silva is still leaning into her broom, her little pile of dust waiting to be disturbed, but she flicks her eyes up at us and nods in a way that seems friendly enough. And then we are making our way single file up the three flights, and though I go up and down these stairs every day without any trouble—fat or no fat—I feel suddenly as if my heart will give out.

"Come in," I say again, indicating my little table and the old armchair and the straight-backed chair where I can still make out my dusty footprints. But otherwise, the room is so clean I barely recognize it. I even wiped out the ashtrays and dusted the coffee table, though I don't remember doing that. It's not just years, faces, that I lose, but what I did earlier in the day: dampening a rag, apparently, and rubbing out ash stains. It was always like that, even when I was younger, whole conversations slipping out of my mind, though I've never forgotten a single book, all of them somehow back on the shelves now.

I dare myself to look at André and he is just standing and smiling. The only time I ever saw him look unhappy was when I ended things. I needed to think of my future, I said, already infatuated with the man I would marry. It was a careless wedding, fueled mostly by the prospect of my husband-to-be returning to the front, and what I was most infatuated with was my husband-to-be's air of authority. I never laughed with him the way I laughed with André, but André was a boy; we couldn't go on forever as we were. "André," I had said. "You have to understand." He'd jerked his head toward the door and told me to leave. We didn't speak again for years. Later, when he found me in my cell—he was unhappy then, too, I think.

I fill three pitchers with water, put the flowers on the end tables on either side of the armchair, and when I turn to him again, he's peering into the box of pastries. He makes a little sound of pleasure and says, "My goodness," as if these were the first éclairs and tarts he'd ever seen.

"I'll just put the kettle on," I say, my voice catching, and then there is nothing for us to do but sit down and stare at each other until the water boils. I insist he take the armchair, pretending I need the other one for my back. The silence doesn't seem to bother him, but I pat my knees for a while—a gesture that reminds me, suddenly, of Pauline—and then I offer him a cigarette, though he never smoked. He lights mine, and then he looks around, taking in the bookcases and the tall windows, the velvet curtain that hides my bed.

"I like your place," he says. "It's lovely, with all the windows."

"Yes," I say. "Thank you. That was a great help."

He looks at me without understanding.

"You gave me this address, referred me to Madame Silva."

"My God, I did, didn't I? I'd forgotten. That was her, downstairs? Madame Silva? I'll need to say hello on my way out." He doesn't mention how they were acquainted, or how he'd learned she had a studio to rent, but now he is full of chatter, recalling people we both knew, the conversation of everyone who grew up in Caen. I'm too nervous to pay attention to most of what he says.

The kettle whistles and I get up to make tea, but instead all I do is turn the stove off and come back to my chair. He's asking after Geneviève now, as if he knows that they're related. Pauline and André were much closer in age than he and I were, and suddenly I wonder if *he* is Geneviève's father. I assumed it was Raphaël, the way Pauline found every excuse to make elaborate pastries for him—and Raphaël was the ladies' man, much more than André—but it could just as easily be André.

I ask him: "Are you the uncle or the father?"

He laughs. "One sister for each brother, don't you think?"

I laugh, too, the people we once were seeming, for a moment, as harmless as dollhouse figures to be positioned and repositioned any way we like.

"I was in Paris when your niece—our niece!— was conceived. Raphaël told me about her—he was so proud of her musical talent." He shakes his head, smiling. "What made you think I might be the father?"

"Oh," I say, shrugging. "Nothing. I don't know." I was in the Salpêtrière when Geneviève was born; I didn't see her until she was six months old and when I did, I blurted out that she had Naquet eyes. Speech was still difficult for me. I couldn't remember what was or wasn't polite to say. Pauline turned red, so I knew for certain then. "I'll have Geneviève's youngest for the summer," I say, to change the subject.

"You have a summer place?"

"In Brittany—a village not far from Nantes."

He smiles. "We have a place on Ile d'Yeu. My wife and I."

I didn't know he had a wife. I'm embarrassed that I didn't think to invite her, but where would she have sat? "You have children?" I ask, as casually as possible.

"No," he says, and something in me gathers, funnels down: I need to tell him right away about Bernard. Someone should know. I might as well have killed Bernard with my own hands. Everyone showed me such pity, the young widow losing her son in the Orne, but what did widowhood have to do with it? I barely knew my husband; if it weren't for the wedding photo, I wouldn't remember what he looked like. And Thérèse? Flesh of my flesh, but she was barely six weeks old, and I have no memory of her face. Bernard was the love of my life, the child who was given to me to keep. I try to imagine him pulling me toward a carousel—I have a photo of him riding a painted elephant—only I can't remember the day it was taken. When I picture him clearly, he's in the river. Sometimes I think I see his shadow, slipping in the reeds, but I know I've made that up. I was still asleep then.

"I killed him," I say. But have I said it? I can't hear my own voice and the light in the windows hurts my eyes. My throat swells shut and the hot light presses in, too close. Someone should pull the curtains. He's watching me, not saying anything, and I want to get up, leave now, but I can't move, my face suddenly drenched with tears. The silence goes on and on, and the light keeps shifting, blurred and sparkling and then dark, as if we'd woken up in the middle of the night. My face sodden. I'd like to slap someone, this is intolerable, these tears—over what? What has happened? My mind is a blank.

"Chouchotte," he is saying, and for a moment, I can't remember his name. André.

"Chouchotte. Listen to me. Chouchotte. I was there. I was with you. Listen to me."

He crouches in front of me, holding my hands, and I want to push him away. He shouldn't see me like this, an old woman with a runny nose.

"Listen to me."

André, I think, over and over, so I won't forget.

"I saw you. It was the fourteenth of July picnic. Half the town was there. Listen."

What is there to listen to? The room is bright and dark by turns, the temperature rising and falling.

"You closed your eyes for an instant, that's all. What happened was terrible, but you're not to blame. Why shouldn't you close your eyes for an instant, with everyone there, watching the children?"

Why has he come here? He is still crouched in front of me, still holding my hands. We were lovers once—does he want me back?

"Chouchotte," he says, and it strikes me that my name—my nickname, "Chouchotte"—is meant to quiet someone. Sh-sh. It's funny that this never occurred to me before, and it makes me laugh, but he doesn't laugh back. He looks upset, as if he wants me to hush, but that never stops a person's laughing fit, it only makes it worse.

"Chouchotte."

I can't control myself, I'm laughing hysterically, though I can't remember what set me off. It feels good to laugh, my breath rising and falling so helplessly—and suddenly I hear him, my Bernard, his own high, sweet laughter joining mine. I keep laughing because he's laughing, we go on and on, setting each other off, until we're spent, and then I feel him throw his arms around my neck and rest his head on my shoulder. It's the first time I've been able to imagine him this way, his fierce heart against mine, and it's exactly as if he's here, in his navy-blue shorts and his sailor shirt, his thin little body giving off a faint odor of wild carrots.

"Chouchotte?"

If I keep my eyes closed and breathe deeply, I can still smell Bernard, feel his breath on my neck.

"Chouchotte . . ." Anxiety rises in his voice, a kind of despair, but if I open my eyes and speak, Bernard will vanish.

"Look at me."

Please, I think, *stop.* I ought to be ashamed: André has shown me nothing but kindness and I have caused him nothing but trouble. *Bernard,* I think, but it's hopeless now. I open my eyes into a moment as bright and sharp as a blade. My apartment scrubbed clean. André squeezes my hand and I can see the relief wash over him, so I squeeze his. "Sit," I say, though it hurts to speak. "Please. Have a pastry."

He smiles a little, a tired smile, and sits back in the armchair. He lifts a raspberry tart from the box and takes a bite. "This is lovely," he says, sadly, and for a moment, I think we're both sad for the same reason.

"Do you still paint?" I ask, not knowing what else to say.

He chuckles. "Still poorly. Do you remember, Chouchotte, how I struggled to position your hands and wrists?"

"Oh, André," I say, without thinking. "I didn't treat you well."

"Nonsense." He pauses a moment and then he flashes me his old, boyish grin. "You taught me a great deal."

"Well!" I manage a smile. "You give me too much credit."

"Not at all. You're much kinder than you realize," he says, lightly, and the air wavers, every molecule touching me beneath my heavy, old woman's cotton.

THE SEX APPEAL OF
THE FRENCH

I told my aunts I was training for an expedition in the Himalayas. I was sixteen, I smoked half a pack of cigarettes a night, and I'd convinced Miss Deyton, the PE teacher back home, that I had my period three weeks out of four so I wouldn't have to play sports. The aunts believed me. Even Miss Deyton, who didn't want to bother with reluctant players, had required some finessing: a week of headaches, nine-day periods, five days for my iron levels to go back to normal. Plus, I was salutatorian, which made Miss Deyton more susceptible to my lies. But the aunts were my French aunts and I'm half American. They thought I could barely spell my name, but they believed me about the Himalayas. A skinny sixteen-year-old with no muscle tone, on her way to Kathmandu.

It was the summer of 1976 and I was staying with my aunts on the coast of Brittany for the entire three months of my vacation. The days were tolerable only if I spent almost no time with my mother's people—Tante Françoise, Tante Chouchotte, and my cousins, who divided their time between waterskiing and studying for national exams. My high school in North

Carolina didn't require studying during the school year, much less the summer, and I hated water sports.

What I liked to do was wander along the cliffs overlooking the ocean, having imaginary conversations. Now and then I'd pause for a cigarette, or take a picture with the used Leica I'd gotten for my birthday; sometimes, I gazed out at the people on the beaches below and imagined what it was like to be them, but mostly I talked to myself. I could fill day after day like that. At home, when my father blew up because he couldn't find his car keys or something in the house broke down, he always told me I could help the most by staying out of the way. I was happy to oblige. With the cousins, I'd have had to spend a lot of time pretending to get their jokes or failing to understand the waterskiing instructions. I was supposedly bilingual, but in French I couldn't catch the subtleties and I came across as mildly retarded.

I wasn't even sure where the Himalayas were, or if Kathmandu was part of them. The best that could be said of North Carolina schools was that they weren't in Mississippi. But even if we'd lived in New England, in some tony Boston suburb, I would have been clueless about the Himalayas. I could ace a test, but I retained no facts, and have no sense of direction. I can't consistently say which way is left and which is right. A wire might be crossed in my brain, but when I was young it seemed more profound to me than that: I wasn't in the world enough to know its shape.

The nice thing about a body of water, of course, is that as long as you stick to the shore, you won't get lost. All along the coast of Brittany there are small, sandy coves, and above the sand, black cliffs; above the cliffs, winding through pale green saltbush, are miles of dirt paths overlooking the sea.

I was walking along those paths one day when it came to me that I had no idea at any given time whether the tide was coming in or going out. People died at high tide. They wandered down onto the rocks and got stuck, were battered against the cliffs. The way tides worked was the sort of thing, like left and right, that didn't stick in my mind. Still, I loved the waves, all that water pulling away, dragging the sand deep into the ocean, and then rolling back, rising and slamming onto the rocks, crashing and collapsing in a ribbon of foamy light. I'd tried to capture it on film, I'd sketched it, written poems about it. I wanted to know what the waves *meant*. Sex? The passionate life I imagined for myself? My fucked-up family with their explosive, circular fights? I was salutatorian mostly because of my grades in English. I loved that everything meant something else, that what was all around me might be a metaphor.

Of course, what I really wanted was a boy-friend. Someone pining for me back home, or someone I was about to meet. Lucy, my best friend at home, my only true friend, said there was nothing wrong with my looks, no reason I couldn't keep a guy, but I was the one-date queen. I'd hang around some cute boy, let it slip that I was half French, and he'd light up. There seemed to be some confusion in the minds of boys, some crossed wire of their own, so that when I said "French," they heard "blow job." Gangly and flat-chested, I could get any boy to ask me out, but the minute he touched me, I froze. I was desperate to lose my virginity, but this was the era of *The Joy of Sex*, a book I studied almost daily, and all those ways to please your lover seemed like instructions I might mess up.

Anyway, the French didn't think it was sexy to be half American, and I wasn't likely to lose my virginity on the coast of Brittany. The incredible thing, more surprising than any lie I got away with, is that I'd chosen to spend the summer with the aunts. I could have done any number of things—a couple of things, anyway: ring up groceries at the A&P, spend the summer in Paris with my mother—and I had chosen this. A pair of gulls flew up past me, vanishing into the glass-blue sky, and then dove suddenly toward the waves, cawing and screeching as they plummeted. *This is the most beautiful place in the world,* I thought, but I wished I had stayed home.

When I was little, my mother had left me in Brittany every summer. She wanted me to enjoy the seaside, the way she wanted my older siblings, sent to relatives in the mountains, to enjoy hiking. She herself spent every summer in Paris. After nine months in America, where no one understood her accent, she needed the cafés and streets of her youth, she needed her own beautician. Our father stayed home in North Carolina and played his cello. Every summer, I wept for days, insisting that I didn't need the salt breeze, I didn't need to be a good swimmer, I just needed my mother. I outgrew the weeping eventually, and the aunts found me a little less intolerable—nothing since the war was worth crying over—but they still thought I was gloomy and slow-witted.

Then, when I was fourteen, old enough to get a summer job, my parents said I didn't have to go to Brittany anymore, and I applied for work at the A&P. Mr. Burnett, the manager, gave me raises every month, said I was the best cashier he'd ever had. I might be working there still if Joel Caruso, the pimply stock boy, hadn't kept trying to touch me. I wanted a boyfriend, but talking to imaginary boys had given me impossibly high standards. Joel, sidling up between the crates of produce and brushing against me, was not what

I wanted. When I turned sixteen, I asked to go back to France. *Come to Paris with me,* my mother said, now that I was old enough to make my way around the city on my own, and I said, *Yes.* And then: *No.* It hit me, I want to say, like a wall of water. I thought it would be easier to find a boyfriend at the beach, easier not to have my mother looking on. I must have sensed, too, that Paris would break my heart, that three months alone with my mother, in her own world, would be too much.

"Why the Himalayas?" the aunts had asked that morning.

"It's a part of the world I've always wanted to see," I'd answered, wondering again where the Himalayas were.

"And you have a group to go with?"

"Yes," I said. "A group. An international expedition group."

"Why not the Alps? Why do you need to go to India?"

India, I thought, and said, "Oh, the Alps, too. I'd love to go to the Alps. Actually, I think the group is planning a trip to the Alps next."

I never stumbled over lies the way so many people do. They flowed out of me, a parallel life. I lied because it was easy, and much more interesting, to move between two story lines. I never felt as if the official story—the "real" one everyone might agree on—was any more deeply true than the imaginary one.

I reached a little promontory that jutted way out over the beach, and I stopped, picturing myself at the top of a snowy peak, lean and sunburned, carrying an old rucksack. On the cover of *National Geographic*, an old, grainy, black-and-white photograph of me, alone, on a needle-thin peak. *Polly Miller, the first woman to climb Mount ____. She was accompanying her lover, the photographer Tomas Seligman, as he fled from the Nazis. Tomas Seligman perished soon after this photograph was taken, but Polly pushed on alone, braving the elements and the altitude so she could publish his work posthumously.*

Tomas had loved me so much. He had brown hair and a mustache, much like Tom Selleck, and no one understood him the way I did. He couldn't believe how beautiful I was.

Kids at school asked me if I ever got my stories confused, but, really, how could you? They didn't know about Tomas Seligman or our flight from the Nazis, but they knew about the excuses I made to get out of things, and the stories I made up just to see what people would believe, and my capacity for deception did a lot to make up for my being salutatorian, and flat-chested, and still a virgin.

The green waves turned white in the sun, cresting and collapsing. A thin, dark-haired man stood in the surf up to his knees, smoking a cigarette, flicking the ashes into the water. He looked twenty, maybe older, and I thought he was the sort of man I'd like, quiet and observant. I imagined us together: how we'd sit side by side, our feet dangling over the edge of a cliff, passing a cigarette back and forth. My stomach tightened, registering the awkwardness and thrill of our first encounter. Then he dropped his cigarette in the water and swam out toward a trio of bobbing heads. The four of them returned to shore, and I saw that he was the father, herding his three little girls to gather their things and go home. I kept walking. I had no desire to go down into the water. It was cold and I didn't like the sticky way you felt when you got out, and I didn't like being inside the motion of the waves. Besides, I was a terrible swimmer. Too weepy when I was little to jump in the waves with my cousins, I'd sat up on the beach, filling buckets with sand because the aunts didn't like idle children.

A motorboat roared past, pulling a skier, water rising behind him like an enormous, foamy wing. The skier was too far away to recognize, of course, but I thought it must be my cousin Jean. The boat was red. I was pretty sure my cousins' boat was red, and Jean was a champion skier. I liked Jean. I'd had a crush on him when I was little, and still hoped he thought well of me. Good-looking and capable like all my cousins, he was a couple of years older than me, and nicer than the rest. Once, he told the others to leave me alone when I was crying, and sometimes he encouraged me in a friendly way to join them in the water. He even talked to me about my mother. My mother used to ski, and he admired her skill. When she brought me to the aunts, she'd spend a couple of days with us, working on her tan and going out on the water. She'd lean back one-handed, laughing, an angel in all that glittering spray.

I never saw my mother laugh in America. Our pleasures baffled her. Peanut butter, for example, that greasy, gluey staple. So much *excessif*! The shopping centers, the packaged snacks, my father's long nights in his studio. My parents didn't fight, but they didn't need to. My siblings—Pete, Louise, Evie—did it for them. Once, Pete busted Evie's jaw, and Louise and Evie regularly scratched the skin off each other. Still, none of their fights compared to my mother's homesickness or my father's coldness.

My father hated the seaside the way my mother hated the States. *What's the point?* he asked. *People broiling like pigs on a spit.* He might have enjoyed walking along the cliffs the way I did—he liked exercise—but he was the principal cellist of the North Carolina Symphony Orchestra, and he had no patience for ordinary life. It amazed me that he knew what people did at the beach. There was a sign on the door of his studio, only half-joking: SILENCE—GENIUS AT WORK. When had he had time to observe a crowd of beachgoers? When he wasn't playing his cello, he was composing or reading; he rarely joined us for meals. We were too noisy, he said, implying that our mother couldn't discipline us, which was true. The older ones were always clamoring for *things*. A color television, a freezer full of ice cream, trips to Belk's for new clothes. My mother dressed beautifully, but *if you have lived the war,* she said, *you do not waste.* She had a single, exquisite, black-lace bra she wore every day, two silk scarves, a pearl necklace and an amber one, three or four dresses and sweaters, a diamond ring. Still, she'd give in to my siblings' demands. Afterward, she'd be in a terrible mood, insist that one time they give her peace, but they couldn't. They'd fight over the rights to every new purchase, getting louder and louder, until my mother shut herself in her room. Even now, with my siblings grown and living on their own, they dropped by on the weekends and started right in, fighting over whose version of some childhood memory was correct, who was going to inherit our mother's ring.

An old, topless woman on the beach was handing out sandwiches to a group of children, and I watched them awhile, wishing I'd brought a snack for myself. Near the picnickers, a younger woman—the children's mother?—lay sunbathing in an orange two-piece bikini. Only the old seemed to go topless, I thought; the young women all lay quietly in beautiful two-pieces. The smallest of the children ran toward the young woman, calling to her to look at something, but she waved him away and rolled over onto her stomach.

The only thing that kept my siblings quiet was my mother's war stories. Sometimes even our father would stick around for those. "A Frenchwoman speaking English—now that's a pretty sound," he'd say, standing in the doorway.

We asked for the same stories over and over: the danger of listening to the radio; the proper way to skin rabbits and sew their pelts together for coats. How to make coffee from corn. After the war, she told us, she'd sifted through the Allied soldiers' garbage for food. Her voice was soft and musical, and I'd think how special we were, with our mother, who had lived the war, and our father, who was so brilliant. I might joke with Lucy about my crazy, fucked-up family, but I meant crazy and fucked-up like the Greek gods. We would have been all right if we could have remained suspended in those stories forever, but America, with its plentiful stores, its blinking lights, its jingles, kept calling us down.

My sister Evie had had it the worst. Pete shoplifted what my mother did not give easily, and Louise, beautiful like our mother, always had a boyfriend to buy things for her. Only Evie didn't know how to game any system. She'd wanted TV and ice cream and she'd wanted our mother's love, too, and she never understood that it was one or the other. Evie looked like me, or I looked like her—all pale angles and freckles—but she didn't know how to lie. She didn't know how to play the heroine in her own imagination.

Much younger than Pete-Evie-Louise, who'd been born in a three-year rush, I learned by watching them, and asked for nothing. I didn't need to—by the time I came along, the color TV played all day long, the freezer was stocked with ice cream, Sara Lee, Tater Tots. *You are nice,* my mother said, stroking my hair, and I leaned into her. Beneath her Nina Ricci, she smelled salty, like the waves, the wet, black rocks.

Until I was five and a half—much older than Pete-Evie-Louise when they were sent to the mountains—she kept me with her in Paris for the summer. We'd lie together in the sunny bed in her stepfather's apartment, voices from the street filtering in through the balcony, and that was all we needed for entertainment, the sunlight, the scraps of conversation, my body curled into hers. We'd get up late, go to the Luxembourg for the merry-go-round and then to her beautician's. Monsieur Schwarz, who ran his salon out of his apartment, was the best beautician in all of Paris, my mother said. I loved his apartment, full of American luxuries: soft toilet paper, a refrigerator, a television. He laughed when he saw me, gave me a bag of candies, and said my mother was his most beautiful client. I waited in the living room while my mother and Monsieur Schwarz went in the back room, where he waxed her legs and eyebrows and fixed her hair. Sometimes, I sat by the door, listening to her strange, soft grunts—the waxing was very painful, she said—until she came out, her skin oiled, hair down her back.

The path curved again. There were no more old women down on the beach, but now the young women were topless. I tried to see if anyone was flat and bony, but they all had delicate bodies with full, barely fallen breasts.

Lucy, who'd slept with six guys by the end of junior year, teased me for gawking at people. Apparently, I walked through the halls of our school, staring at everyone, so absorbed my mouth nearly hung open. *I swear to God, I can't take you anywhere,* she'd say. *Between the talking to yourself and the gawking, you're like someone who never got properly socialized.* Then we'd both laugh about how inappropriate I was and that might lead to how stupid everyone else was when you thought about it, and we'd give up on school for a while and go smoke behind the gym. Lucy was pretty much at the bottom of the class, despite all the times I stretched back in my chair or dropped my paper so she could look at my answers. Despite how truly smart she was. She said the problem was not that I had imaginary friends, the problem was I thought I was imaginary; I didn't realize people could see me, all bug-eyed and gaping.

My mother had been a watchful, solitary girl herself—a serious violinist, which was how she'd survived the war. Her family home in Normandy was destroyed on D-day, but my mother was in Paris, auditioning for the conservatory. It was a mild, breezy day all across France, a good day for a bombing raid, and as she drew her bow down for the first note, she was overcome with nerves, but she kept playing. It took her a month to learn that her mother and one of her sisters had been buried in the first round of Allied bombs. They dug up her mother's body, but all anyone could find of the little sister was an arm.

She met my father a year after the armistice, in a church near Notre Dame, at a performance of a Mendelssohn string quartet. They'd both heard the concert from the street and slipped in at the end of the first movement. By the beginning of the third, my father, towering over her in the back of the church, had taken her elbow as if he'd known her for years.

• • •

The topless women sat in beach chairs, reading, smoking, dozing. Now and then they looked up to scold whatever children were nearby—*Allez! Arrête! Ça suffit! Go on! Stop! That's enough!* I felt their irritation all through my body, as if I had a slight fever, as if I were five and six and seven again, and they were my aunts. But these women paid no attention to me, up on the cliffs, and after a while the feeling vanished.

Beyond the beach of topless young women was a fully nude beach, and I sat on one of the benches along the path to settle in. Only the women were naked—the men wore Speedos—but from where I stood (close enough to study the shapes of breasts, too far to hear much of anything), I understood that this beach was all about sex. There were no children, and the women stood straight, flat-bellied. The men watched. One man pushed a woman into the water, laughing. I might tolerate the cold and the salt and the waves, I thought, if I had a boyfriend to tease me that way, and then I thought of the parable we'd read in English, about the hermit who lived on a hill overlooking a village. He never went down to the village, but when, because of some trouble or another, the villagers moved to a new valley, far from the hermit's hill, the hermit packed his belongings and traveled until he found them, whereupon he climbed a hill and built a new hut overlooking the new village. I loved that story.

I got up again, and was suddenly mortified by my halter top and jeans cutoffs. Frenchwomen never wore cutoffs or Indian-print halter tops. What had I been thinking? I should have spent a few days in Paris before I came to Brittany, asked my mother to take me shopping. She didn't object to shopping in Paris the way she did in the States. You rang a bell to be admitted into a store, suffered the disapproval of the shopkeeper whose afternoon you'd interrupted, and bought a single, beautiful item that would last your whole life. I *had* asked her if I could go to Monsieur Schwarz's before I went to the beach, if he'd shape my eyebrows and give me a nice haircut. I wasn't trying to be rude. I suspected he was more than her beautician, but I still wanted to believe he had a salon in his back room, that he was *primarily* a beautician. She snapped at me in a way she'd never done before. "You do your eyebrow by yourself," she said, her eyes glittering. "The young people anyway—they prefer the natural look, no?"

My throat felt tight, but I didn't want to walk all the way back to the house to change. Into what? All my clothes were obviously American. This was how the world got you, grabbing you by the ankle and pulling you under. You were walking along, talking to people in your mind, having a fine time, and suddenly you realized how stupid your outfit was. The world turned watery around me and then I imagined Lucy, with her American sensibilities, cringing at all the nakedness, and I was fine again.

Beyond the beach of naked women was the beach of naked men. This was even more fascinating, but the view wasn't as open. I would have had to lie down on the rocks with my head hanging over the beach to see much of anything, and I tried to draw the line at obvious, deliberate spying. The path wound away from the cliffs, into the dunes, so I left it to climb the rocks. I loved jumping from rock to rock, coming upon the sudden clear pools, the narrow coves you could leap across. I wasn't worried about the tides. To be afraid of death, you must be convinced of your own existence.

In English class, when we got to all the world being a stage I'd thought, *Yes,* picturing myself in the audience. At the center of the stage is my family's living room where my mother sits, telling the story of how her mother and baby sister were killed. Pete and Louise are trying to kick each other without anyone noticing, but Evie leans toward my mother, as if she means to lay her head on my mother's lap, unaware that this is not the right moment to do so: my mother is lost in her own world, and we must not disturb her. My father, bored by the actual story, has closed his eyes to better hear the cadence of my mother's voice.

As my mother speaks, she gazes down at her palms. She seems to hold the events of June 6 in her hands, as if D-day were inside a snow globe: There is her family's house, there are her mother and sister. When she shakes the globe, it isn't snow but rubble that rains down and now she can see it, what she missed that day by being out of town, how the house was crushed; she can make sense of it, can stop and start the crumbling at will.

I sit breathlessly in the audience. I can't tear my eyes from the snow globe, though I'm just as terrified of Pete's and Louise's kicking, Evie's longing, my father's indifference. Those are real lives, I think, strutting their hour upon the stage.

After a while, I found myself in the sand; the tide must have been going out while I was rock-hopping. I had no idea how I'd gotten there or where I was, but when I looked up, I saw that I was on the beach of naked men. All around me were Frenchmen—so much finer and slenderer than Tom Selleck—lounging, strolling along the beach, staring out at the horizon. I couldn't breathe. Before I could figure out how to get back up on the cliffs, a bald man with a goatee wheeled around and asked what I was doing. His penis rose faintly from the tight nest of his pubic hair, and I said, *Je cours.* I'm running.

French people did not jog in the 1970s, and in that way I was wholly French. I was instantly winded, but once I'd made a spectacle of myself—a badly dressed American girl loping through a gay men's beach—the only thing to do was to move on as quickly as possible, which wasn't quick at all. My feet slipped in the sand, and though I tried to keep my eyes on the shoreline, I seemed to see them all, those fine-limbed men with their sinewy muscles, their dark blurring genitals. It wasn't a big beach, but it took me days, it seemed, to cross it, and the whole time, I was ashamed the way you can only be ashamed in dreams, as if I were the naked one, and everyone else were fully clothed. Every last man stopped what he was doing and stared as I ran past.

I slowed down a little when I reached the beach of the naked women. Among the men, I'd been an outrage; here I was just a misfit. Two women, one almost as flat-chested as I, the other with breasts the size of her head, stared at the fringe on my shorts, but no one froze at the sight of me, or no one froze for long. I glanced enviously at all the lovely collarbones, the slender hands, the unembarrassed breasts, and wished more than ever that I looked French. *This will be funny later,* I thought, trying to console myself, and I pictured the crowd I could entertain with my story. Then a better image presented itself to me: I was opening my locker at school, and a boy was leaning in to hear what I was saying. *Sure. I've spent time on nude beaches. Of course. In France.*

A nun in full habit was walking toward me, conversing with a man in a wet suit. The nun smiled at me, and I smiled crazily in return. I was on the regular beach now, where the fully clothed and the half naked coexisted; there was no farther beach to run to.

I imagined Lucy touching my arm as I leaned over to catch my breath. *Honest to God,* she laughed, *I cannot take you anywhere.*

Stairs were carved into the cliffs leading up to the dirt path, and I headed straight toward them. Two couples were sunbathing near the base of the steps, a picnic basket at their feet. One of the couples lay quietly, but the other was flirting, the boy pulling at the girl's bikini top while she batted his hand away. An ordinary teasing couple, I thought, and I stopped, transfixed: the girl raised her head, the boy motioned out toward the beach as if to say, *See? Lots of women have taken their tops off.* She lay back down. He pulled a strap down one shoulder. When he fumbled with the clasp, she shrugged him off, pulled her strap back up, and they began again.

My eyes stung. *This* was what I wanted. Not to go topless, not even to look French, but to have a boyfriend who flirted with me, who'd repeat the same preliminary gestures over and over. A boy with infinite patience.

He couldn't take his eyes off her. Every time she shrugged him off, he bent and kissed her neck, and I was sure he knew her more intimately than any other boy knew a girl. I walked straight toward them, as if I meant to stand right above them. Men and women kissed everywhere in France; it didn't occur to me that they might want privacy.

But something was wrong. The boy was older than I thought, hair on his back and shoulders; the other couple was a mother and her preteen son. Just as I realized it was the girl's father flirting with her, trying to take off her bikini, she lifted her head. I stood three feet away. She looked at me with an expression of pure rage, wild black eyes in an acne-covered face, and I ran.

I wasn't winded anymore. It seemed I could run for the rest of my life, and never grow tired, but still, at the top of the stairs, I stopped. *Lucy,* I thought, but there was no one there: only the murmur of voices from below, and the wind in the saltbushes.

Once, the aunts had taken my cousins and me to a farm somewhere. An electric fence surrounded a herd of cows and when the aunts weren't looking, we dared each other to touch it. I hated the way it felt, and I loved it, too: that sudden, dark, wounding surge. I kept touching the fence after the others stopped and it made them laugh, as if my love of getting shocked were a crazy American thing, like my accent, and the way, jet-lagged, I slept for days after my mother dropped me off with them. What I craved was the way I could feel my whole body, all the way to the edge of my skin.

I sat on one of the stone benches along the path and stared at nothing. Something was wrong with *me,* with the day, with my whole stupid plan of finding a boyfriend, but I didn't know what it was. Old people strolled past with their dogs, and now and then a family made its way down the steps, carrying beach chairs and umbrellas. None of them would even glance at the girl and her father, I thought. They had what they wanted. Why should they waste time gawking?

But it obviously wasn't *contentment* that would keep the other beachgoers from looking. It was a sense of propriety. If a man was violating his daughter, they mustn't watch.

I pictured myself going back down the stairs, scooping up a handful of rocks and throwing them in her father's eyes. I'd grab that girl and take her far away. I ran through the scene over and over, as if I could wish it into being and the next step—what the girl and I would do next— would reveal itself, but nothing came to me.

Keep me company, Lucy would say, when she failed an exam. It didn't change anything—she still wouldn't get into college—but I always stayed with her. You can always keep someone company.

I went down the stairs then and took a spot on the beach near the girl. The tide was way out, wet sand almost to the horizon, littered with seaweed and driftwood. No one swam at low tide; they spread out far from one another and lay still beneath the burning dome of the sky. Her father might tell me to leave—I sat so close to them I could hear their breath, I imagined they could hear mine—but the only indication he gave of my presence was to stop his hand in the middle of his daughter's back.

For the rest of the afternoon, I sat with my knees pulled up to my chin, willing the girl to know she was not alone, willing her father to die of shame. I didn't want to gape at the girl, but I didn't want to look away, either, so I pretended to search the horizon for boats. I kept hoping to see Jean out on the water again, as if, in the midst of skiing, he might sense me here, drop everything, and what—? What could he do?

Later, I knew, the girl's father would finish what he'd begun—he'd take her top off, her bottom, too, maybe—but as long as I sat with her, he wouldn't move. The tide would stay out, the sky hold still above us.

LES MUTILÉS

Where are the signs instructing us to give up our seats for the war-wounded? PRIORITÉ AUX MUTILÉS DE GUERRE. There's the little picture of the rabbit getting his fingers pinched, to warn children about the train doors closing, but nothing for the war-wounded. Nothing to remind us of our manners.

I like giving up my seat. It's such a small thing to do: a nod, a moment of eye contact, if the man still has his vision. *You who hold our suffering in your body. Please, sit.*

Hundreds of us hurtling together beneath the city, and no one seems troubled that the signs are missing.

But I've lost my mind. This is a new train, they don't post the signs anymore. There are grandmothers who can't remember the war. All that's left are the anniversary celebrations. Twenty-five years. Fifty years. Sixty, sixty-five, seventy. Poster-sized photos of the Liberation all over Paris and coffee-table books with those snapshots of people dancing in the streets. My son, Pete Junior, told me that at the war memorial in Caen, you can buy a box of D-day candies. This was an aside. His main point was that I should visit the memorial. I haven't been back to Caen since '44. Why would I want to see what they've built upon the ruins? He told me about the different rooms of the memorial, how interesting it was that the whole thing was underground, and I felt myself flow out of my body, as if I were relieving myself in the street, which I have done. At the end of the war, I stood on rue Soufflot in broad daylight, nineteen years old, my mother, sister, grandmother dead, and the pee streamed down my leg, so warm it felt good.

I looked up at Pete Junior, at his handsome head of gray hair, as he described the exhibits, and thought, *I have taught you nothing.* I used to tell the children stories, over and over, the same ones: my home, bombed on D-day, my sister's shattered body. The children gathered around me the way they gathered around their shows on television, loving the violence, the excitement. I believed my stories were instructive: *Give thanks for your good fortune; if the Nazis are at the door, lie.* But they learned nothing, squabbling over who got to sit next to me, who got the last cookie.

The missing signs. For a moment, I was confused, forgetting what year it was. I wouldn't say I'm senile, unless it's senility to slide around the decades, lose track of where you are on the time line. Ninety-one next month. I'm tired. (But so impressive, my doctor says, since he has nothing to offer me for the exhaustion. *You still ride the metro! Imagine that!*) I still know who I am, who the others are. But here is an interesting development: I can no longer subtract. I have to ask someone—a neighbor, a grandchild, whoever happens by—to balance my checkbook. I can add, but I cannot take away. You'd think it would be the reverse, that at the end of my life, with everything falling away, subtraction would be my only skill. That test for senility, the backward counting, I'd fail it, but what does that tell you? I am still myself, if bereft of certain words, of a child's skill with numbers.

In place of the signs, the brightest of advertisements. We might as well be in the States. I never think of myself as an American, though after the war, I married one. Lieutenant Peter Miller. We had known each other for a month. A tiny wedding in a tiny church on rue Saint-Jacques, with my stepfather giving me away, his gaze as empty as a POW's. He'd looked that way since D-day. It was 1946, Paris cleared of barbed wire and debris, but the streets still full of beggars. Children and amputees. The morning after the wedding, I boarded a ship with Peter, and five days later, I found myself in a land of supermarkets and state fairs. I thought of the empty stores back home and my mouth filled with bile. It took me fifty years to become a U.S. citizen, and I only did it, finally, because Peter insisted. For inheritance purposes, he said. Dying of cancer and he was worried about my future! Maybe he did love me, I thought. I felt the way I had in the fifties, when he put a bomb shelter in our backyard. Who would want to survive an atomic bomb? But I thanked him anyway. He had meant the shelter as a kindness to me. Besides the bomb shelter and the inheritance business, there wasn't much—we barely spoke to each other—but I sometimes think of those two things, wonder if I misjudged him.

Rémy was furious that I'd become an American. It made me laugh. I spent every summer in France with Rémy; Peter was glad to be rid of me for a while. "Rémy," I said, "I'm still French. It's just for the house, so I can sell it." But I shouldn't have laughed. His face fell, and all day I couldn't comfort him. "Rémy, I have loved you all these years. Only you." When the children were small, I took them with me to France and sent them to the countryside to stay with relatives. June to September, Rémy and I had Paris to ourselves. "Rémy," I said, "what does it matter, a piece of paper? You are the man I love." I was only a dual citizen, it wasn't as if I'd given up being French.

He was too angry to answer, and for a moment—I'm ashamed to say it—I thrilled to his disapproval as though I were a young girl. Standing in his kitchen while he opened a plate of oysters for us, I thought, *He wants me all to himself.* You'd think I would have had enough of other people's anger, after all those years of the children fighting like animals and Peter in a perpetual silent rage because I couldn't control them, but it was different with Rémy. I'd never seen his temper. He sliced the edge of his thumb and kept right on prying open the shells, blood streaming all over the oysters' gray, slippery bodies, and then he popped the whole dozen, one after the other, into his mouth, wiped his lips with the back of his hand, and left the room.

He'd always been so reserved, so proper, that I'd half thought he didn't care deeply about me. What an idiot I was! He held doors for me, pulled out my chair, walked on the outside of the sidewalk—courtesies Peter would have laughed at—and when the children were still young and Rémy drove us to the airport each September, he squeezed my hand, but he did not kiss me good-bye in front of them. I told the children he was my hairdresser. I should have said a distant cousin, because then I had to go on pretending for years that there was nothing strange about a woman's hairdresser accompanying her to the airport. I built it up—*There is no one more important in a woman's life than her stylist!*—as if all I cared about in this world were a good cut and color. I would have gone gray in my thirties if I hadn't been so busy maintaining the illusion of myself as a French beauty. Even now, I rinse my hair with vinegar to keep the white from yellowing.

"Rémy," I said. "I don't love Peter."

There's nothing to stop Rémy and me now from joining our resources and moving in together. Peter's been dead for twenty years and I divide the year equally, six months in North Carolina, where the children and grandchildren can visit me in my handicapped-accessible retirement complex, and six months in Paris. But Rémy has his own apartment off Avenue Émile Zola and I have a fifth-floor walk-up on rue Casette. I don't know what the children would say if my Paris address changed. They're still so volatile. They think I only come here for family, and even that unnerves them. They have very particular ideas about how I should be cared for. *Stay home, Mama. Mama, you can't keep going to France, the trip's too much for you. The Meadows has everything you need.* The Meadows! A horror of look-alike bungalows, each with its own wheelchair ramp.

I have to agree to wear the alarm necklace when I'm in the States, call one of them every night when I'm in France. They blame each other for everything that happens to me—for my arithmetic errors! *How could you fucking forget to look over her checkbook?* Past middle age and they still yell profanities at each other. I did not raise them very well.

They say I wasn't "there" for them, but it was

hard to pay them enough attention when they were growing up. They needed so much! Toys, television, doughnuts. Like giant furnaces I could not stoke fast enough, though, in fairness, there were times I barely stoked them at all. I was too sad.

It's ridiculous to take the metro. I don't know why I insist upon it. Someone always gives me a seat, of course, but I can't read the signs rushing past. I have to ask where we are, and then everyone is so worried. *Are you all alone, Madame? Is there no one to help you? Where are your children?*

It never occurred to me that marrying an American meant I'd have American children. But nothing comes into focus when you're young. You rush forward through life and it's all so noisy—the war and the end of the war, the world in ruins, and the American soldier taking your arm in the back of the church where they are playing a Mendelssohn string quartet, the F minor. The soldier tells you in English how pretty you are, can he take you dancing?

Nearly everyone is dead, so why not? Dance with him, let him slip your dress off your shoulders and enter you. He had no idea I was a virgin, and though it didn't hurt, I wept, so grateful for his body. His clean, living body in my arms. I wanted him to come back inside me, over and over and over again, I wanted to stay in that bed with him forever and he laughed finally. "You French, it sure is true what they say about you, isn't it?"

I hated him then, of course, but what could I do? Hate him or love him, I could not tear myself away from his living, pulsing, clean body.

And then, suddenly, I was in Raleigh, North Carolina, with four children and an enormous refrigerator full of pasteurized cheese and iceberg lettuce. For myself, a Valium. *Valium.* The same word in French and English, such lovely syllables, like water, or a bell. A valley. *Vallée.*

I was so scared that first year in America. I could understand Peter, his pronunciation almost like the English I'd learned in school, but I could not understand the others. *Y'all. Wanna. Yonder.* We lived three miles from a shopping center, in a brick house with a closed gazebo in the back where Peter played the cello. He went out there before dawn and did not return until nightfall. I used to walk to the stores along the smooth, cement sidewalks, trying to understand where I was. The big, swift automobiles and the wide lawns; the blond schoolchildren in the windows of the yellow buses; and the housewives in their bright clothes, watching the street.

The first time I went inside the A&P, I wandered the aisles, tracing my fingers over the labels on all the jars and cans. Ketchup, peanut butter, Spam, pork 'n beans, Hershey bars, coffee. I was supposed to buy food for Peter's dinner, to think of what he'd like and how I might prepare it, but it was my sister I was thinking of, Françoise. She was home on D-day, but she didn't die. She crouched in the garden and watched the house collapse on our mother, sister, grandmother; and while she crouched, I stood before the faculty of the National Conservatory in Paris, two hundred and fifty kilometers away, playing the violin.

Françoise, with her long black braids, and her body like an eleven-year-old's, even at fifteen. She didn't get enough protein during the war. Afterward, she developed tuberculosis, had to spend a year in the Alps in a sanatorium. She was our mother's favorite.

I stood in the A&P and thought of the apartment in Paris where Françoise and our stepfather were living now—he'd crouched next to her that day in the garden—furnished with things they'd dug out from the rubble: an embroidered tablecloth, my mother's sewing kit, an old bell, a photo album. I left the A&P with nothing.

My heart was racing so fast when I got home that I had to disturb Peter in his gazebo. I was shaking, drenched with sweat. "I cannot," I said. "What? What can't you?" "I cannot," I answered, over and over. He led me back into the house— the sky so brilliant it hurt my eyes—and then he made me drink a glass of water and lie down. I interrupted him another day, he was practicing a Haydn concerto, and he set his bow down and sighed. "If this is going to become a habit." Then he put me to bed, went out to his car, and drove away. When he returned, he had a small bottle from the pharmacy. "Dr. Jameson saw me without an appointment," he said, so I would appreciate the trouble I'd caused. "You're to take these when you get upset."

He encouraged me to play the violin, and I did sometimes, but I had mostly lost interest. I'd never really been interested, to tell the truth. The audition at the conservatory was simply a way to get out of the house. To get away from my mother's watchful eye, my stepfather's disapproval.

It's nice and warm in the metro, that's part of what I like. Everyone sweating and fanning themselves and for once it isn't because I've turned the heat up too high. Besides, I like seeing the young people, with their gadgets and tattoos. Bobbing to music no one else can hear.

Peter would have loved an iPod. All he wanted all day long was music; it didn't bother him that I was not like other wives. He had me at night in his bed, and he was perfectly happy not to interrupt his playing with a meal. If I could remember to bring him peanut butter sandwiches at noon and six, he was satisfied.

And then, one afternoon, after we'd been

married two years, he came into the house to get something. "Oh, Jesus," he said, because I was sitting at the kitchen table, crying. "Are you out of pills?"

I shook my head, surprised that he would ask. I always cried in the middle of the day—those long, bright, empty hours in front of the picture window, looking out over the bright and empty lawns.

"Well, Jesus, Jenny, why are you crying?"

He couldn't say *Geneviève*.

I tried to think of a story—bad news from home that I could use as an excuse for my tears—but I couldn't think of anything terrible enough. "Bad luck," he'd said when I'd told him about D-day. "What a mess."

"Did you actually take your pill?"

I nodded. "I cannot—it is difficult to do things alone," I said, finally.

"You want a maid?" He looked around the kitchen, which was easy to clean, since I never cooked. "What for?"

"I'm sorry," I said. "That is not what I mean." I did not want someone to get down on her knees and scrub my floor, I wanted a woman to talk to, someone besides my neighbors: Mary O'Brien next door said she was dying to go to Paris, had I ever been to the Champs-Elysées? *Chomps-Elley-zays*. Joanne Greene across the street *had* visited Paris before the war, but her hotel room was small and dirty, the shopkeepers were rude, and she could not believe that a civilized people still used squat toilets.

I followed Peter's gaze around the kitchen: the starched gingham curtains, the big refrigerator, the "Home Sweet Home" needlepoint his mother had made. "What I am trying to say," I said. "I would like to go home."

He laughed, but he was not smiling. "A god-damned divorce? Is that it, Jenny? I thought you were a Catholic."

"No," I said, "I do not want a divorce." I was pregnant, though I hadn't told him yet, but he was right, anyway: I was a Catholic. I could hardly bring myself to say the word "divorce." "A visit. I would like to visit home."

He chuckled then, more easily. "Jesus, Jenny. You had me scared. A maid would be cheaper, though. You sure a trip is what you want? I can't do both."

I'd only had to ask. He said I should go for the whole summer, because I hated the heat so much and it wasn't worth the expense for a short visit, anyway. In the weeks leading up to my departure, I stopped crying, I didn't need so many pills, I even cooked. Peter didn't like my cooking—the first meal I made for him was sautéed sweetbreads and he pushed them away, explaining that his people didn't eat organs—but it didn't matter. He preferred his peanut butter

242

sandwiches in his gazebo to any proper meal, and I was happy to eat alone. I was sick in the mornings, but by midday, I was as ravenous as I'd been during the war, only now I could eat whatever I wanted: pork roast, cold tongue, veal, cake. I gained two kilos in two weeks.

I bought presents for Françoise and for my older brother, Simon, who'd left home when I was still a child: a dress for Françoise—white dotted Swiss with a red belt—and a book about Frank Lloyd Wright for Simon. For my stepfather and my aunt Chouchotte, books about de Tocqueville.

I wasn't afraid to go up in an airplane, to feel the sudden lift in my body, the tilting side to side. The moon shone in the window, and beneath the moon, a field of clouds. All night long, flying over the Atlantic, I kept thinking, *I am happy,* and I couldn't sleep. I wanted to tell my mother how happy I was—to tell her I was pregnant, which I still hadn't told Peter—and I was sad that I couldn't do that, but for the first time since D-day, not so sad that I could not be happy, too.

No one was pleased to see me—no, that's not right. At first, they held on to me as if I'd come back from the dead. They were all beautiful, even my stepfather. All waiting for me at the airport: my stepfather, Françoise, Simon, Tante Chouchotte. We could not speak for a moment, and then, suddenly and all at once, their voices! I had gone such a long time without hearing them, without hearing any French at all. I was so happy to walk out into the gray morning, to smell the air, so much lighter and softer than the air in North Carolina. I could barely form my words, I was too happy, too unused to speaking French. And the shops on the way to the apartment, the shopkeepers rolling up their grates; the street cleaners sweeping the gutters; the old, beautiful buildings—I wept openly, though I had been raised not to make a spectacle of my feelings.

But their warmth only lasted a few days. I could feel them shrinking from me, from my sudden, careless wealth. The books I'd brought were nice, of course, but the dress was ridiculous. Three sizes too big. Françoise was still rail thin. When I saw her standing in it, the dotted Swiss hanging off her narrow shoulders, I asked her if she'd like to come back to America with me at the end of the summer. She looked away, said nothing. It embarrasses me now to think of how, too late, I tried to mother her.

I'd never been like the others, even before I married Peter. Something had been off about me, the way I looked—pale and blond, like no one else in the family—the way I kept to myself. Before the war, my stepfather teased me about the violin, mocking every missed note; now he barely spoke to me. And yet he insisted I stay with him and Françoise. I would have been

244

happier with Tante Chouchotte or Simon, but Simon was recently divorced, excommunicated— my stepfather would never have let me stay with him—and Tante Chouchotte, who loved me in a brusque, fierce way, had only a single room. So I slept with Françoise, in her narrow bed. Françoise talked to me about the weather, or how we'd slept, or what we'd have for dinner, but she wouldn't speak about our mother, our sister, our grandmother. If anyone mentioned the war, she gave a strange, brittle smile and said how lucky we'd been. And who could dispute her? We were alive.

Every day, my stepfather sat in the living room, reading, and Françoise knitted by his side. Dozens of scarves, gloves, socks, sweaters, hats, as if she lived in terror of ever being cold again. I tried joining her, but my knitting was clumsy, and I could feel her irritation when I dropped a stitch and started over. Our mother had been so good with her hands.

I began to go for walks. Along the river, around the Luxembourg, all the way out to the Bois de Boulogne. In the shifting summer light, America seemed like a fever dream. The shadows of clouds flowed through the trees, golden one moment, dusk green the next, and I drank in the cool smell of the river, forgetting all about Peter, as if I had conceived the child in my belly on my own. I did not have to strain to understand the bits of conversation drifting past: I was as much a part of this world as the paths, the breeze, the deep cold water of the Seine.

One day, walking past a patisserie on rue d'Assas, I saw a young man come out with a baguette. I'd been too sick to eat breakfast that morning, but, struck by a sudden craving, I stared at the bread in his hands as if he were offering it to me. Then I noticed his red hair, his bright blue eyes. I had seen him before, but where? I remembered a bicycle, and suddenly it came to me: an image of him, paused on his bike outside our home in Caen, my stepfather waving him away angrily. My stepfather had wheeled around and slapped my sister Yvonne, and then he stormed up the steps to our house. I couldn't picture Yvonne's reaction—she was so wild she might have laughed—but I remembered the boy's: his eyes like shattered glass, and the color rising to his cheeks.

"It's you!" I said, going up to him. I didn't know his name. Yvonne herself had never learned it. She told me, after our stepfather slapped her, that he rode past our house every day and that she loved him, though they'd never spoken until the instant our stepfather caught them.

"It's you," I repeated. He flinched a little. "You're from Caen, aren't you?" That seemed to reassure him. "My sister," I continued. "Do you remember a girl with long dark braids, watching you from her balcony? The summer of '43."

He smiled then, his whole body relaxing. "Oh," he said. "Yes. Yes, of course I remember. She's your sister? Please tell her—I'd love to see her." He laughed a little. "If I'm permitted."

"She's dead," I said. What was I expecting? That he would take me in his arms and console me? He stared blankly, as if he had no idea what I was talking about. "Our house was bombed," I explained.

"Oh," he said, collecting himself. "Well, I— yes. Yes, of course. My condolences." He turned abruptly and walked away, and I stared after him, watching his long stride, his bright hair, but then, suddenly, he came back. "Excuse me," he said. "What was her name?"

"Yvonne." This time, when he started to leave, I said, "She loved you."

He smiled again. It was such a pretty smile, flashing across his whole face. "Thank you," he said, but the smile was already fading. "I'm happy to know her name."

"And you are?" I asked, to stall him.

He hesitated. "Rémy."

I put my hand out. "Geneviève," I said. "Geneviève Miller."

"Miller?"

"My husband is American. My maiden name was Delasalle. She was Yvonne Delasalle."

"Yes," he said, taking my hand finally. "I knew

your last name—your maiden name—from the mailbox. Rémy Schwarz."

"Oh," I said, embarrassed. Of course we'd known of the Schwarzes—his father owned a men's clothing shop—we'd heard when his parents were arrested. "You're alive," I said, stupidly, still holding on to his hand, though I could feel him pulling away, his calloused palm loosening itself from mine.

"I am alive," he agreed. His face had gone blank again, and I knew I should let go, I shouldn't bother him further, but it seemed that if I could keep him there, if we could just stand on the sidewalk with the day brightening and fading around us, we would be all right. But I could feel his desire to get on with his afternoon, so I dropped his hand, he nodded, and we said our good-byes.

The next time I saw him, he was by the river, fishing. This time, he smiled, reeled in his line, put his pole down. "We meet again," he laughed, and offered me a cigarette, as if nothing bad had ever happened, anywhere. He invited me to get a cup of coffee with him. "A miracle," he likes to say now, "that we should have found each other that day by the river. Out of everyone in the whole city." He never mentions the patisserie.

In the café, we didn't speak of Yvonne. He wanted to hear about America, so I told him about the stores, the food, the wide streets, the damp, terrible heat.

"And your husband?" Rémy asked. "He's not with you?"

"No," I said. "He's a cellist. He needs to practice every day. He cannot take vacations."

Later, he said it was obvious that Peter and I didn't love each other, but he did not imagine that he and I would come to love each other, either. It was pity that drove him to invite me home with him, and when we got there, to the little one-room apartment where he lived by himself, we sat on his sofa and did not speak. The dead were all around us, softer and more commanding than any living thing.

At first, I had no idea what to make of Rémy—of his strange good cheer when we met the second time, or his invitation to go home with him. Apart from the sofa, his apartment was nearly empty: a camping stove, a little cupboard for food, a trunk for clothes, a bedroll. Nothing on the walls, no curtains in the windows. But sun streamed across the floor, and it did not feel gloomy, just quiet.

I didn't know where his parents had been sent after they were arrested, and yet it was clear that they had not survived. His father had been an excellent tailor, his mother a fine seamstress, but Rémy's trousers were torn at the cuff, his shirt was missing a button. Rémy was all that was left of the Schwarzes. If he acted strangely, it was because he didn't know how to be in the world anymore. We knew by then what had taken place in the camps; Rémy would have been forced to imagine it, to picture everything.

We sat for a long time and then, because the light had faded from the windows and I thought Françoise and my stepfather would worry if I didn't come home, I said I should leave.

"Come again," he offered, seeing me to the door. "If you'd like."

Françoise was still knitting, my stepfather still reading. He looked up at me, nodded, and went back to his book. "There's potato soup," Françoise said, indicating the kitchen, and I was sorry that I hadn't been there to help her prepare dinner. I ate a bowl because of the baby, but every bite filled me with shame.

A little while later, the doorbell rang and Françoise jumped up and smoothed her hair.

"That will be your young man," our stepfather said, and I was confused for a moment, thinking he meant Rémy. It was Grégoire, of course, the man Françoise would marry. She had never mentioned him to me.

Every day, Rémy and I sat quietly on the sofa in his living room. We must have done other things, but from those first weeks I remember only the silence of his apartment. I'd imagine Yvonne on the other side of the door, as if, at any moment, she'd burst through. Beautiful Yvonne! She looked exactly like Françoise, with her long dark hair, her black eyes, but there was something about her—her posture, like a dancer's, her long hands, and her fearlessness—that made her the beauty, and Françoise, with her shoulders slightly curved, the sweet one. *Beauty and Kindness.* Yvonne insulted the nuns openly at school, mimicked the Germans behind their backs, refused to obey our stepfather or our mother. "Why can't I go to Paris?" she demanded, when I left home to prepare for the conservatory. "Why Geneviève and not I?" It was ridiculous—I was eighteen, she was barely fifteen, and there was nothing in particular she wanted to study. And yet, it seemed perfectly reasonable: she was bold and capable, and, as I've said, I was just an odd duck, shut away in my room for hours. She'd throw open my door, flop down on my bed, and tell me what she wanted. My pen or my hair ribbons, my little white cardigan. "Yvonne," I laughed. "What will I wear, if I give you my cardigan?" "My school vest," she said, pretending to vomit. "Tell me a story, then, if I can't have your cardigan. Something to console me for the barrenness of my existence."

I laughed again. "You tell a story, Yvonne. Yours are the best."

She sighed. "Once I ran away with a boy on a bicycle." All her stories began that way.

"What was his name?"

"Nicolas? Bertrand? He never told me, but we rode to the tip of Spain. I sat on his handlebars the whole way, and then we took the ferry to Tangier. In Morocco, he traded me for one hundred camels, and then he bought me back for ninety-nine, and we rode our lone camel all the way to Cape Hope."

Françoise dug through the rubble for weeks. Dirt, stone, beams, her hands bloody, her fingernails broken off. That's what I imagine, at least, since she never spoke of it, and neither did our stepfather. He told us only that the bombs had fallen at 1:30 on June 6, that it had taken sixteen days to find the remains, that he'd managed to secure two coffins, so they would not have to go in a mass grave. They had found our mother and grandmother on the very first day; it was Yvonne who took so long, and what they found of her fit in a child's suitcase.

Rémy said even less about the war. I don't know if he was arrested with his parents and escaped, or if he had already fled by then. I started to ask him once, and he drew back as if I'd hit him. I never mentioned it again. He didn't want to hear my stories, either. "That's all finished," he explained. "It serves nothing to speak of it." But his voice was so gentle that I felt as if he knew everything.

The first time he touched me, apart from shaking my hand, we'd gone out to walk and he took my arm. It was raining, an ugly, spitting rain, and he covered me with his jacket, steered me back inside, and put the kettle on. I imagined Yvonne's voice, its sweet, wild lilt, *he bought me back for ninety-nine,* and I started shaking.

He felt my forehead, but of course, I had no fever.

"I should go," I said.

He touched my arm. "Stay."

"It would break Yvonne's heart."

"I didn't know Yvonne," he said.

"She loved you."

"She was barely more than a child," he said.

I burst into tears, and as I sat there, crying, he undid my blouse, took off my shoes, and when we made love, it was nothing like it had ever been with Peter. I remember only light, as if we did not even have bodies.

And then I was back with Peter, in the shocking late-summer heat, with the cars honking and the cash registers ringing and the neighbors inviting me for Jell-O and bridge games. I could have learned to play bridge, I suppose, but I could not bear the cold sugary tea and tiny Wonder Bread sandwiches.

I wrote Rémy to tell him I was carrying Peter's child and I told Peter, too—I could hardly hide it any longer—and I feigned a miserable pregnancy to avoid going out. But the truth is, I loved being pregnant that first time. When my daughter was born, I named her Yvonne. She goes by Evie, but her birth certificate reads "Yvonne."

This might be my metro station. There are nine stops between my apartment and Rémy's, but I forgot to keep count—and now they're closing the doors. Be careful, little rabbits. "Was that—?" "No, Madame," a woman says, too brightly, before I've even named the station. "Two more stops. I'll tell you." When his rheumatism was not so bad, Rémy used to come to me.

Sixty-five years. That's how long we've been together, Rémy and I. I used to dread September, but now I stay in Paris until the day before Thanksgiving. Such a terrible holiday. All those plates of dry turkey and canned cranberry jelly, just as you are served in a hospital. Marshmallows in the sweet potatoes! But the children still ask for stories, and that is always nice.

"There were so many air raids," I'll say. "After a while, we stopped bothering to run to the basement." When the children were small, I could feel their breathing soften, as if I were singing them a lullaby. "We'd simply run to our mother's bed, and then, finally, we stopped even doing that. We were too tired to be afraid anymore, and we slept through the sirens like babies.

"By '44, the Germans were arresting anyone

they suspected of Allied sympathies. And all the Jews, of course, even the ones who'd been French for generations. When the Allies were closing in, and the Germans had caught every Jew they could find, they fled the city. The Allies knew the Germans were gone, but they bombed us anyway. They had to, you see, to disrupt the Nazi communications. Your aunt Françoise, she was just fifteen, and very hungry, but she lifted stones all day after the house was bombed."

Once, I told a different story: "My mother—oh, if you had known her!—she was very different from me. Very strict." They laughed. "And very hardworking. Of course, during the war, we all had to work. Digging potatoes, turnips, carrots. Skinning rabbits and sewing the pelts into coats. My mother could skin five pelts in the time it took me to kill a single rabbit. She was a round, serious woman and she did not tolerate foolishness. But before my father died, before she married my stepfather, she had an affair. Yes, an affair!" I had learned this from Tante Chouchotte, on her deathbed. It was still new to me, the fact of my mother's secret life. "With a doctor, a Jewish doctor. My little, round mother, who went to mass every day, who'd slap you if you cried about anything."

"Far out," Polly, my youngest, said. "Grandma was ahead of her time!" She was sixteen, desperate for a boyfriend. I was about to tell them that my mother's lover was their grandfather, killed at Auschwitz. Daniel Delasalle, the man I called Papa, who died of diabetes when I was five, was no relation. Tante Chouchotte had held my hand, white hair fanned out on her pillow, her face so gaunt that I could almost glimpse the girl she'd been—those high cheekbones and gray eyes, like my mother's. "Docteur Naquet," she said. "Do you remember him?" I didn't. "A terrible womanizer," she smiled, "but a very brave man. He was in the Resistance. You must remember him." I shook my head, wondering if she was making it up. I remembered having the measles and the doctor coming to the house, though I couldn't picture the doctor's face, but there had been a rumor during the war that Chouchotte was hiding someone, a Jew. Perhaps this same Docteur Naquet.

"Geneviève," Tante Chouchotte said. "Listen to me. You don't need to keep checking your children for signs of diabetes. Docteur Naquet was strong and healthy—strong enough to seduce a churchgoer like your mother and a dozen other women."

"My mother? How?"

"I don't know how to say it any more clearly, but it shouldn't be difficult to understand. You have your Monsieur Schwarz after all." I was surprised she knew about Rémy. She slid over in the bed so I would lie next to her. "You have an uncle," she continued. "A gynecologist. I introduced you to him once, a lovely man. Apparently he was saved from the camps by a painting. I don't really know—it made no sense at all when he told me." We were still holding hands, lying together in her big bed. I could smell her breath, the musty, fermented breath of the very old. "I wanted you to know because—" But she had lost her train of thought, murmuring now about horses, a leak in the roof, her bathing suit. If she had not mentioned Rémy, I would have dismissed everything she'd told me. If I'd not suddenly remembered a stranger in Tante Chouchotte's apartment, kissing me hello. *Docteur Naquet.* My uncle.

I wanted to call the children on the telephone and tell them right away about my mother, my father, their great-uncle. I didn't think of them as grandparents, only as Maman, Papa, the Docteurs Naquet. But if my father was not my father, my mother was not my mother. The woman who slapped me when I cried, who said a rosary every night, who lifted the covers on her bed for me— my soft-bodied, stern, devoted mother, dead for thirty years. Who was she? Who was the man who could seduce her, even for an hour?

I did not call the children. I waited until I was back in America, and then Polly said *Far out,* and I thought, we will never be able to communicate. Years later, I did tell them, when they were older and ready to start their own families. To my surprise, they were very kind. Pete Junior said it must have been a shock, and he put his hand on mine. "You're half Jewish," Evie said. "Thank goodness no one knew." I blushed; for a while, that was Rémy's nickname for me: my beautiful half Jew, *ma belle demi-juif.*

That was all so long ago—Tante Chouchotte on her deathbed, Polly's excitement about my mother's sensibilities. When I think of my mother now, I remember only the warmth of her bed; I can just picture Docteur Naquet's hand shaking a thermometer.

Polly has stopped saying *Far out,* except as a joke, but I don't tell her what's truly funny: how every generation thinks it has invented sex.

Just once, I nearly told the children about Rémy. They were fighting about whether or not I should continue driving, and I wanted them to understand—something—but I caught myself in time, my heart pounding.

Impossible to remember Rémy's bright, red-haired innocence! His politics veer to the right now, it's horrifying to listen to him, and his apartment has turned into a fussy old man's bachelor pad.

And yet, the sight of him—there, on the sidewalk, in a sunny rain shower, waiting for me (I don't remember the train stopping, the escalator up to the street)—his softly drooping face, his jowls and his stubble, cane in one hand and umbrella in the other, the stains on his shirt!

"Come, Rémy. You shouldn't be standing out in the rain like this."

Let's go to bed, I think, *and watch the shadow of your curtains ripple across the room. It's enough to feel your old body in my arms, my old body in yours. Enough to have found you down by the river.*

ACKNOWLEDGMENTS

I have been lucky beyond all measure in writing this book. Enormous thanks to my editors, the gifted and visionary Laura Brown and the incredibly generous Terry Karten; my brilliant agent, Alexa Stark; my kind and extraordinarily wise first readers—Judy Goldman, Susan Monsky, Darnell Arnoult, Katey Schultz, and Tommy Hays. I'm stunned by my good fortune in getting to work with all of you.

Huge thanks to everyone at HarperCollins—Jonathan Burnham, Christine Choe, Tracy Locke, Joanne O'Neill, Leah Carlson-Stanisic, Christina Polizoto—and to Jacqui Daniels and SallyAnne McCartin at McCartin-Daniels.

To Jessi and Chris Grass, Adrienne and Atticus Stovall, Jim Grant, Nicolette DeWitt, Giancarlo Toso, Sebastian Swann, Bethany and Lily Rountree, Laurie Smithwick, and my current and former students and colleagues at the Table Rock Writers Workshop, the Great Smokies Writing Program, and Appalachian State University—thank you for everything you have taught me.

To Larry, who makes everything possible—no words suffice.

Deep gratitude also to the North Carolina Arts Council for its support, and to the editors of the following publications, where portions of this novel first appeared in slightly different forms:

Five Points: "The Sex Appeal of the French"

The Alaska Quarterly Review: "The Phony Mother"

Drafthorse: A Lit Journal of Work and No Work: "The Ransom Ring"

Witness: "The Jew & the German"

What Writers Do: An Anthology of the Lenoir-Rhyne Visiting Writers Series: "Liberation"

ABOUT THE AUTHOR

ABIGAIL DEWITT is the author of the novels *Lili* and *Dogs*. Her short fiction has appeared in *Five Points*, *Witness*, the *Alaska Quarterly Review*, the *Carolina Quarterly*, and elsewhere. She has been cited in *Best American Short Stories*, nominated for a Pushcart Prize, and has received grants and fellowships from the North Carolina Arts Council, the Tyrone Guthrie Center, the McColl Center for the Arts, and the Michener Society.

Books are produced in the United States using U.S.-based materials

Books are printed using a revolutionary new process called THINKtech™ that lowers energy usage by 70% and increases overall quality

Books are durable and flexible because of Smyth-sewing

Paper is sourced using environmentally responsible foresting methods and the paper is acid-free

Center Point Large Print
600 Brooks Road / PO Box 1
Thorndike, ME 04986-0001 USA

(207) 568-3717

US & Canada:
1 800 929-9108
www.centerpointlargeprint.com